MOUNTAIN MAGIC

MOUNTAIN MAGIC

•

KRISTIN HUNGENBERG

AVALON BOOKS
THOMAS BOUREGY AND COMPANY, INC.
401 LAFAYETTE STREET
NEW YORK, NEW YORK 10003

PRINTED IN THE UNITED STATES OF AMERICA
ON ACID-FREE PAPER
BY HADDON CRAFTSMEN, SCRANTON, PENNSYLVANIA

Special thanks to Jody Brand,
whose beautiful ranch in Walden, Colorado,
inspired the setting for this book.
All the peaceful hours of fishing on his property
have been much appreciated.

I would also like to thank all of my family
for their help and support,
especially my three wonderful aunts:
Pam Skersick, Carol Lockwood, and Colleen Flack

Chapter One

The alarm shrilled loudly, waking Teal from a deep and dreamless sleep. Groaning at the rude awakening, she slid to the other side of the bed and fumbled with the clock. Once she'd switched off the alarm, she sat up and tried to rub the sleep out of her eyes.

All Teal really wanted was to crawl back under the covers and escape from her life. She'd never been the type to be depressed before, but everything that had happened in the last few months was weighing her down. With a heavy sigh she opened her eyes and looked at the clock. She grimaced at the illuminated numbers, which revealed that it was 5:30 in the morning. Today she was going to have to put her life back in order, and the monumental task seemed like more than she could handle.

"One thing at a time," she reminded herself. "I'll just take care of one problem at a time until eventually all my problems will be solved." She

1

laughed at the absurdity of that statement, and the sound came harshly even to her own ears. "The first thing I need to do is to quit talking to myself," she said aloud.

Her bedroom was softly lighted by the sunrise flooding through the windows. The oranges and yellows of the sky created a soft and inviting atmosphere in the room. Teal walked to the windows and gazed at the sun sitting low on the horizon. It looked like a ball of fire as it began to warm the land and sky. There was nothing like watching the sun rise to put life back into perspective. There was always hope in a new day.

Feeling a lift in her spirits that hadn't been there in quite some time, Teal turned away from the windows and walked into the adjoining bathroom. The face that looked back at her from the mirror showed no sign of the strain she'd been under. Her long blond hair was still as shiny and soft as it had always been, and her green eyes were as bright and vivid as ever. She ran a brush through her hair and pulled it back into a simple ponytail. The last few weeks in the mountain sun had left a rosy pink on her high cheekbones and a flattering darkness on her skin. She had a natural beauty that reflected the healthy lifestyle she led.

She quickly slipped into a faded pair of jeans and a comfortable T-shirt before heading down to the kitchen. The rich aroma of coffee brewing reached her as she made her way down the stairs and across the dining room. She smiled as she swung open the kitchen door and saw Millie preparing breakfast at the stove.

"Good morning, Millie," she called warmly. Millie Carpenter had been her family's housekeeper as long as Teal could remember. Now she was the only family Teal had left.

Millie turned at the sound of Teal's voice and smiled in return. "Well, good morning. You're up and about early this morning, aren't you?"

The warmth of Millie's voice cascaded over Teal's frazzled nerves like a waterfall, soothing her immediately. Millie had been like a mother to Teal ever since her real mother had died in a massive train accident when Teal was just five years old.

Teal walked across the kitchen and gave the older woman a hug, which Millie vigorously returned. "Thanks for being here, Millie," Teal said softly.

Millie stepped back and gripped both of Teal's arms strongly. "You know I'll always be here, as long as you need me. We'll get through this together. Just like we always have." Millie was two inches taller than Teal's five feet, five inches, and a good twenty-five pounds heavier than her 125 pounds. Teal had a boyish and athletic figure with a good deal of strength of her own, but Millie's grip hurt nonetheless.

Teal ignored the pain and answered, "I know you're right. We'll just take everything one thing at a time."

"Right you are. And we'll start with breakfast," Millie said as she turned back to the stove. "Pour yourself a cup of coffee and I'll have your French toast ready in no time."

"French toast?"

Millie knew exactly what she meant. "Now don't you be arguing with me about how many calories you're eating. You've got lots of hard work ahead of you, and you're going to need energy. Not to mention the fact that all you seem to do is exercise. Fat doesn't have a chance to rest on your bones, girl."

Teal laughed heartily as she poured herself a cup of coffee and sat down at the kitchen table. Light was flooding in from the beautiful morning outside, making the kitchen homey and cozy.

"Sure feels good to hear you laugh again," Millie remarked as she put butter and syrup on the table.

Surprise showed clearly on Teal's face as Millie's remark registered. "I guess it feels good, too.

There hasn't been much to laugh about around here lately.''

"Don't I know it. But your father wouldn't want you moping around forever. He'd have wanted you to get on with your life."

Teal's eyes turned misty at the mention of her father. She and Millie and almost the entire town of Walden, Colorado, had buried him just two days ago. Paul Berringer had been a strong man, though not strong enough to fight the cancer that had consumed his entire body. Paul had spent the end of May and most of June in the hospital in Denver until he died quietly in his sleep. He'd been on so much pain medication that he hadn't even recognized Teal at the end. She had been with him almost every minute that the doctors had allowed, and now he was gone. She had brought him home to Walden to rest beside her mother in the cemetery at the south end of town.

Paul had lived his entire life northwest of Walden on a two-hundred-acre ranch that he had eventually inherited from his father. Teal had grown up there, and she loved every inch of the place. After college she had gone into teaching, and for two years she had taught physical education in Greeley, Colorado, a three hour drive away. At twenty-five years old she was not only an orphan, but unemployed as well. A new tax law had decreased the budget for education so badly that many teachers in Colorado had been left without jobs. Teal was only one of many.

Teal shook her head and tried to dispel the gloom her depressing thoughts had brought back. She loved this ranch as much as her father had, and now she was going to learn how to run it for herself as well as for Millie. "Yes, you're right, Millie. Dad would want me to get on with my life. I think he'd be happy to see me back here on this land he loved so much. It just doesn't seem right that it was his death that brought me back home." She had come back to visit frequently, but she hadn't called the ranch home since she was eighteen.

"No, it doesn't," Millie agreed. "But the important thing is that you are home, and you're going to keep this place going. It sure hasn't been the same since your father got ill."

Teal was shocked at the anger in Millie's voice. "What do you mean? Joe has been taking care of the place, hasn't he?" Joe Andrews had been helping Paul with the work for about eight years. He lived in a trailer home down by the river and was paid well for the time he spent keeping the ranch in working condition.

"Depends on what you mean by 'taking care of the place,' " Millie said with disgust. "Here, your breakfast is ready."

The French toast smelled heavenly, but Teal wouldn't be sidetracked. "What has he been doing?" A sinking feeling settled in her stomach as she thought of Joe Andrews. He had always given her the creeps. He seemed nice enough at first glance; it was just the way he looked at her. His eyes seemed to devour her. He was outwardly handsome with curly dark hair and a powerful physique. At six feet tall and 180 pounds he made a very forceful impression. Too much so for Teal's liking. He seemed to think he was a real lady's man, but he did nothing for Teal. In fact, though she hated to admit it, the way he looked at her sometimes scared her to death. One of the things that she had been dreading most was going out to talk to him about the ranch and what needed to be done.

Millie's answer confirmed her fears. "It's what he hasn't been doing. Namely, working."

"He hasn't been working," Teal echoed dumbly. The thought of confronting him was daunting, to say the least. Even more so if he thought he could do nothing and live there for free.

"He hasn't irrigated any of the hay fields or pastures in about three weeks, which might be all right in a wet, cool summer but it's been hot and dry now for weeks. The grass has hardly grown at all; there's not going to be much there to cut for winter feed. The cows have eaten down the pastures that they're in, but he doesn't seem to care. I saw him drinking a bottle of whiskey down by the river yesterday afternoon.''

''Great,'' Teal commented as she gripped the edge of the table in agitation. ''That's all I need. He tried to be friendly and concerned at the funeral. He even told me how I didn't need to worry about the ranch. He was going to take care of everything. And all the time he's been sitting around doing nothing.''

''Well, you'll fix that,'' Millie commented with utter confidence. She thought of Teal as a daughter, and was extremely proud. She knew that Teal could do whatever she put her mind to. She was a strong woman, and Joe Andrews didn't stand a chance against her. Millie would be there to help her as much as she could; after all, this ranch had been her home for twenty years. She'd come to live there when Teal's mother had died. Paul and Teal had become like family. Millie had one brother that lived in Kansas, but she didn't see him very often. She and Paul had grown close very quickly; he was more like a brother to her than her own. They had never had the typical employer/ employee relationship. Millie had helped Paul get over the loss of his wife just by keeping his house in order and taking care of his daughter. He had returned the favor by making her feel like one of the family. Adjusting to his absence was going to be difficult for both women.

Millie's vote of confidence buoyed Teal's flagging courage. She began to feel angry at the way Joe had just let the place slide when no one had been around to do anything about it. She was certainly going to do something about it now.

"Where are you going?" Millie called after her as Teal marched out the back door.

Teal called back over her shoulder, "I'm going to set some things straight around here."

"Wait a minute," Millie protested. "You haven't eaten your breakfast."

Teal stopped and looked back through the screen door. "I'm sorry, Millie, but this just can't wait any longer. I'll eat something later; I'm really not that hungry, anyway."

"Oh, all right." With a heavy sigh she continued, "I'll bring you back something good for dinner. I'm going down to Fort Collins to shop today. Do you need anything?"

"No, nothing special. I'll see you when you get back."

Teal turned and began walking down the lane to the river. It would have been faster to take her dad's pickup, but she wanted some time to decide what she was going to say. Besides, the air was so fresh and clean that the exercise would do her good. Walden was a beautiful little town nestled in the Rocky Mountains. As far as the eye could see, pastureland, lakes, and rivers spread out in lush abandon, making it one of the most popular fishing areas in Colorado. Teal's ranch was ten miles northwest of the town, and her 200 acres of rich grass meandered along with the north fork of the North Platte river. There were impressive mountain peaks stretching all the way to the horizon on all sides. Teal knew that she would never have found a more beautiful place to live if she'd stayed away.

She had inherited the ranch from her father, and she was going to do the best she could to keep it going. She owned it free and clear; all she had to do was make enough money to live on and to pay Millie and Joe a salary for their help. Her income would come from raising calves and gradually adding to her herd. Her father had always sold the calves when they were about a year old. The market was up now, which encouraged Teal. She'd helped her father enough to know what needed to be done, but she'd been away from it so long that she felt just a little bit rusty, and more than a little afraid of the responsibility. Even though she didn't particularly trust Joe, he knew what he was doing; his help would be invaluable. There were some things that she just wasn't strong enough to do by herself.

The key was going to be finding a way to work with him. It was obvious she was going to have to keep an eye on him if she expected him to do anything. She came around the small bend of the hill that her own house sat on and gazed at Joe's trailer. It sat on a high point about 200 yards from the river and was surrounded by the pastureland that supported Teal's herd of cows. She could faintly hear the river flowing, and the sight of willows on the banks brought back a rush of memories. She and her father had spent many happy hours down here just fishing and talking. Her heart strained as she thought of how much she was going to miss him.

She caught sight of Joe moving around in the barn and made an effort to swallow the lump in her throat. Right now she needed to keep her mind on business. The barn sat along the same ridge that Joe's house rested on and was only about fifty feet from his door. Teal forced herself to keep walking until she stood at the open doors of the barn. She had to wait while her eyes adjusted to the dark interior, allowing Joe to see her first.

He set his bottle of whiskey down beside a bale of straw before walking over to meet her. His steps weren't exactly steady, and the overpowering smell of stale alcohol reached Teal before she saw him. When her eyes finally focused on him she was aghast at the sight. His shirt was unbuttoned, revealing a dark and hairy chest. His clothes were filthy, and there was at least a two day growth of beard on his face. Teal's mouth dropped open as she stared at him. She'd never seen him like this before. She was too shocked to speak.

"What brings you down here?" Joe asked as he belched and scratched his stomach.

Teal was totally revolted. "What do you think you're doing?" Her plan had been to keep her temper in check, but she hadn't expected anything like this. Her anger began to spiral as she looked at him. How dare he! Her father hadn't even been gone a week and this man thought he could just turn into a lazy, drunken bum. That he thought he could still live here made Teal see red.

"What do you mean?" he slurred as he belched again. "Can't you see I'm working."

"Working? You call drinking yourself into a stupor work? How dare you sit on my father's land and drink in the middle of the day while there's work to be done. Just who do you think you are?"

Immediately a change came over him as anger at her words began to build. He stood taller, and a menacing look came into his eyes. Teal had never seen anything so evil-looking in her life. Involuntarily, she stepped back. His hand whipped out and grabbed her arm before she could step any further away. He had a grip of iron that made Millie's hold of earlier that morning seem like the brush of a fly in comparison. "Who do I think I am?" he mocked. His eyes narrowed to small slits as his lips pulled back across his teeth. "Who do you think *you* are, miss high and mighty? You think you can come down here and tell me what to do?" He shook her arm forcefully, and Teal cringed away in horror. "Let me tell you something: I could run this place with both hands tied behind my back. I've been doing the work around here for years without any help from you or that father of yours neither. Working my butt off for what? So he could give this place to you? I have a right to my share. I'm the one who kept this place what it was. What does he give me for all my work? A bonus—a lousy, measly little bonus."

Teal didn't know what she had expected, but it certainly wasn't this. Trying to swallow her panic, she answered, "You certainly couldn't have expected him to leave it to you. I'm his only daughter, his flesh and blood. Of course he would leave it to me. It's been in my family for three generations." She had softened her voice and was doing her best to calm him down and placate him with something.

It didn't work. If anything, his grip on her arm tightened. It felt to her like he was crushing her bones between his fingers. "I had a right to expect more than a bonus!" he screamed as his anger escalated. "A guarantee to work this place, a lifetime lease, something to show appreciation for all I've done. What do I get? I get his goody-two-shoes daughter, who thinks she's too good for the likes of me. That's what I get. I'll tell you something," he said as he leaned into her and leered at her, "I think I'll take more of a bonus than money."

Teal was beginning to be very frightened. His look said that he had every intention of harming her. She knew she was going to have to do some fast talking before something awful happened. "I'll give you a guarantee," she stammered. She steadied her voice before continuing; she knew that showing her fear was the worst thing she could do. He wanted to scare her. "I'll give you that lifetime lease, if that's what you want. Now, please let go of my arm; you're hurting me."

He threw his head back and roared with laughter. The stench of whiskey assailed her and combined with her fear to make her feel like throwing up. She clenched her teeth to hold it back as he abruptly quit laughing and leered at her again. "No, I think

I'll take my bonus. The one your father handed to me on a silver platter.''

''What are you talking about?'' Teal asked as calmly as she could. She knew she had to keep him talking. She was half a mile from the house; Millie wasn't likely to hear her. More than likely she had already left to go shopping anyway. There wasn't another person around for miles. She was going to have to get out of this herself. She had taken self defense courses as part of her major in college, but nothing had prepared her for this.

He laughed again at her question, and the stench made her knees feel weak. He grabbed her other arm and pulled her in close to his own body. ''I'm going to give you a taste of a real man, honey.'' His laugh rang in her ears as he roughly captured her lips with his own. He had done it so fast that she hadn't had time to react. Now she began to twist and turn, trying to get away from his wet and slobbering mouth.

He bit her lip hard enough to make her gasp with pain. Even though Teal had lifted weights for years and was in phenomenal physical condition, his strength overpowered her. Panic seized her as twisting and struggling only seemed to incite him further. Some logical part of her brain realized what was happening and began to take over. Her panic subsided, to be replaced with an awesome rage. She was going to fight him to her death if she had to. Recalling what she'd learned in her self defense courses, she brought her knee up into his groin as hard as she could. His breath rushed out of him as he doubled up and pulled away from her.

She gasped for air, but she knew that she didn't have any time to waste. She aimed another kick at his groin, but he was already clutching himself in pain and his hands deflected the blow. Because of his superior strength, standing and fighting him wouldn't be the smartest thing to do; she realized that her best bet would be to run. Turning quickly, she pushed off to sprint away. He lunged at the same time and grabbed her lower leg, tripping her up. She landed hard in the dirt, immediately turning over and bringing her right leg across in a swinging arc, her heel catching him full in the face.

She'd kicked him with enough force to send him sprawling into the dirt. Again, she bounded up with the intention to run away, but he was just as fast and caught her. He spun her around and drew his hand back to punch her full in the face. She saw it coming just in time and ducked, but the force of the spin threw her off balance, and again she fell. Joe recovered quickly and fell on top of her, his weight effectively pinning her arms and legs. There was nothing she could do.

"Spunky little thing, aren't you?" he laughed.

Teal was horrified. She had struck him with two effective blows and yet he was lying on top of her laughing. He didn't seem to be in the least bit affected. He was probably too drunk to feel any pain or too angry to let himself notice. Either way, she knew she was in a lot of trouble.

There was nothing she could do as he dropped his lips to hers in a brutal kiss that was meant to punish. One moment she was gagging and the next she was lying free of his weight as he was lifted off her and thrown aside. She scrambled to her feet as she watched a total stranger kick Joe square in the face. Joe's body arched up and fell back slowly. Teal watched in fascinated horror as his body moved in apparent slow motion; it looked just like the movies, she thought. He landed spread-eagled on his back and didn't move again.

Teal gasped for breath as the man turned to face her. She backed away as he walked toward her; she'd never seen him before and she was too mixed up to even think of trusting him.

He stopped and opened his hands in a gesture of peace. "I'm not going to hurt you," he assured her. "My name is Nick Marcus. Felix Marley at the cafe in town told me you might be needing a hand out here. That is, if you're Teal Berringer."

Teal didn't answer right away; it was all she

could do to catch her breath. She felt like she'd just run the Boston marathon. She was shaking from fear and the effort she'd expended. Nervously, she smoothed back her hair and tried to calm down. She needed the time to recover and to study the man before her. He wasn't quite as tall or as heavy as Joe but he looked like he was in good shape. He was lean yet well-muscled, and his shirt stretched taut across a powerful chest and shoulders. He had a narrow waist and long, long legs. His light brown hair was wavy and long enough to brush across his collar, but the thing that affected Teal most was the soft expression in his chocolate-brown eyes.

He was watching her with such a look of concern. No one had ever looked at her like that before. It was obvious that he wanted to help her, but he didn't even try to come any closer. Teal was grateful; the last thing she needed was comfort. Too much caring and concern when she was hurt had always made her fall to pieces. That was the last thing she needed, and he seemed to know it. The fact that he did was intriguing to Teal, to say the least.

She finally caught her breath, but still she continued to stare at him without answering. To break the silence he repeated, "Are you Teal Berringer?"

This time his words snapped her out of her stupor. "I'm sorry. Yes, I'm Teal. Who did you say you were?"

"Nick. Nick Marcus. Felix said you might need some help out here. That's why I'm here. Nobody answered at the house, so I came down here looking for you. Are you okay?" He was speaking slowly, as if he wasn't sure she understood him.

"I'm fine," she answered as she nervously smoothed her hair back again. "I'm sorry, I must seem like a total idiot to you. It's just taking me a while to recover. Going from fighting for your life to being perfectly safe in a matter of seconds is rather hard to adjust to. Thank you for what you did. I was fighting a losing battle by myself."

Nick was impressed. The man had obviously been intent on raping her; he'd seen enough to know that. And yet, here she stood calmly thanking him for his help. The tremor in her hands as she smoothed back her hair was the only sign of any inner agitation. If he'd thought about it, he would have expected a woman to fall apart after an ordeal like that. Her courage was amazing. "You don't need to thank me," he answered softly. "I'm just glad that I came along when I did. Are you sure you're okay?"

Teal gently explored her lip with her fingers to see what kind of damage his bite had done. The skin hadn't been broken, but it was beginning to swell a bit. "I'll be okay," she assured him again. "All he had time to do was bite my lip, but it's not serious. Do you think we should do something with him before he comes to?"

Nick looked back at Joe lying in the dirt. "I don't think he'll be coming around anytime soon. From the smell of him, I'd say he'll be out from the alcohol for awhile. We should call the police, though."

"Oh . . . yes . . . you're right. I'll go in and do that; there's a telephone in his trailer."

"Okay. I'll stay out here and watch him." Nick sensed that she wasn't going to trust him immediately. She'd been through too much in one morning for that. He was perfectly content to give her the space she seemed to need. It surprised him, though, that she didn't seem to need a shoulder to cry on. Most of the women he knew certainly would have.

She nodded her agreement and turned toward Joe's trailer. Thoughtfully, Nick watched her walk away. She certainly wasn't the woman Felix had led him to expect. Felix hadn't mentioned how incredibly beautiful she'd be. Her slim hips had a comfortable swing to them as she walked, and her luscious blond hair fell down her back in complete disarray. She had the confident walk of an athlete.

He didn't know exactly what he had expected; now that he thought about it, she looked like the type to work outdoors. She'd already proven how much strength and stamina she had. This was certainly going to be interesting.

Chapter Two

The sun was high overhead by the time the police were finished with their questions. Teal had pressed charges for assault, but Joe probably wouldn't be in jail for very long. The judge would most likely release him on bail by the end of the day. Even with Nick as a witness, the police didn't think she should try for attempted rape. They had advised her that assault would be her best bet for a conviction. Teal had listened to them; all she really wanted to do was get it over with. At least she wouldn't have to deal with him every day anymore. Now she had to figure out what she was going to do without him.

Nick stayed behind after the police left to make sure that Teal was all right. It was obvious how worn out she had been by the ordeal. "Looks like you could use some lunch. It'll be my treat if you want to go into town."

His words made her realize that she hadn't

eaten anything yet today. She wished now that she'd eaten her French toast; she was starving. "You're right. I guess I missed breakfast this morning. I wanted to get that confrontation over with while I was good and angry. Well, at least it's over with."

"I'm sure Felix would be happy to cook us up something to eat," he said, trying to lighten her mood. "He makes a pretty good hamburger."

"I'm so hungry I could eat a horse. Come on inside and I'll see what Millie left me. The least I can do is feed you after all you've done for me."

"You don't owe me anything."

It hit her finally, that he said he had come out looking for a job. With everything that had happened she hadn't paid much attention to his story. "You said that Felix sent you out here. You can tell me about your qualifications while we eat." She turned and headed toward the house, knowing he would follow.

Nick had to smile as he shook his head at her stubbornness. She obviously wasn't the type to take no for an answer. He followed her into the kitchen and looked around. Something about old houses had always touched him. They looked like homes instead of simply dwellings. The atmosphere in the kitchen further reinforced his feelings. White curtains billowed out from the window over the sink. The entire kitchen was painted in white, even the cabinets, making the dark oak table stand out in stark relief.

"Go ahead and sit down. I'll just find some things to put on the table. Is cold fried chicken okay with you?"

"Sounds good. I guess I'm pretty hungry myself." Nick pulled out a chair and sat down to watch Teal move back and forth to the refrigerator.

Teal put out two plates and some silverware and then sat down at the end of the table. "Did I miss anything?"

"Looks like more than enough to me."

"Help yourself."

Nick served himself a generous helping of chicken and potato salad, as well as a couple of rolls. He poured himself a glass of milk and then stopped to watch Teal out of curiosity. She seemed to have forgotten that he was in the room at all as she filled her plate and began to eat with a voracious appetite. He smiled to himself at the sight.

Teal felt his gaze and looked up. A light pink dusted her cheeks as she put down her fork and sat back. She returned his gaze for a moment before saying anything. She hadn't noticed before how good looking he was. It wasn't so much the way he looked; it was more the way he looked at you. There was something about his eyes that was totally riveting. A mixture of intelligence, sadness, and compassion showed on his face. She found herself just wanting to stare at him. Making an effort to break the spell she seemed to be under, she said, "I guess you think I'm a real pig, shoveling food into my mouth at ninety miles an hour."

"Oh, I think you exaggerate. Surely forty miles an hour is more like it."

He smiled at her with such charm that she burst out laughing. "Are you going to make a citizen's arrest? You know the speed limit out here is only thirty-five."

"I don't see Gomer Pyle around anywhere, so I think you're safe."

Teal laughed again. "I guess you must have grown up with the Andy Griffith show too."

Nick lifted one eyebrow. "Didn't we all?"

"I don't know, but I'm sure there are some deprived people out there who haven't seen it."

"I used to watch all of those old shows. Gilligan's Island was my favorite. It's a good thing I don't have time for television now; they don't make shows like that anymore."

"No, nothing like the good old days." Teal smiled ironically. "I sound like my father; he always used to talk about the good old days."

"I was sorry to hear about your father."

Teal was touched by the sincerity in his voice. Most people gushed on and on about grief and how time would heal the pain. Somehow, Nick's simple statement conveyed more feeling than any of those banal statements possibly could. Teal was intrigued; she'd never met anyone like him before. "Thank you," she said simply.

"This sure is a beautiful ranch. It must be heaven to live in the mountains like this. I've seen almost every state in the U.S., but Colorado certainly takes the cake."

Teal smiled at his enthusiasm. "Where do you come from?"

"I grew up in Oklahoma. I learned about ranching from my father. He operated a thousand acres. It was big, but not big enough for all four of us."

"Four of you?"

"I have two older brothers. Don't get me wrong; I love all of them. But working with them full time was too much. We all have our own ideas, and most of the time mine didn't match with theirs. So I'm working my way around the country, seeing how other people operate. I've learned a lot in the last five years."

Teal could tell from the wistfulness in his voice that he was glossing over the story. There was probably a lot more to it than he had admitted.

"So when Felix told you there was an opportunity to work out here, you thought you'd come check it out. Is that right?"

"Well, he wasn't completely sure there was an opening; he just said it was worth a try."

Teal had known Felix all her life. He'd run the cafe in town ever since she could remember. He wasn't the type of person to trust any stranger that happened into town. And there were a lot of people that came through for the fishing and hunting in the area. It surprised her that Felix would send Nick out here. Was it possible that he knew of her aversion to Joe? Or had he seen through Joe all along? Whatever the reason, he had inadvertently saved her life today. "Have you known Felix long?" she asked.

"No. I just met him today when I was having breakfast. He thinks the world of you, you know."

"I know. That's why it surprises me that he would send a total stranger out here."

"I'll give you my parents' phone number if you want to check my story." His voice softened as he added, "Is it so hard to believe that other people would see what kind of man this Joe Andrews is?"

"No, of course not. He's given me the creeps forever. It surprised me that my dad didn't see it. But what I meant was, it surprises me that Felix would trust you instantly. Especially since he doesn't know you.''

Nick raised one of his eyebrows again. ''Does it really?''

Teal studied him for a moment. She wondered if he knew how devastatingly handsome he looked when he raised one eyebrow like that. No, he didn't seem to be at all aware of how attractive he was. There was nothing cocky or arrogant about him. She sighed. ''No, I guess it doesn't surprise me. There's something honest about you. Do people always trust you on sight?''

''Most of the time. It's usually pretty obvious, don't you think? I mean, for those of us who develop our gut instincts and then follow those instincts.''

''Those of *us*?'' she asked in surprise. How did he know if she fit in that category or not?

''Are you saying that you don't have an intuition about people?'' he said as he cocked his eyebrow again.

''No, I was just wondering what made you think that I did.''

Nick smiled. ''My gut instincts tell me that you do.''

Teal smiled back. He was right; she knew that she could trust him. It was just a little bit disconcerting to have someone be able to read her so well. "So, I have a ranch hand position opening up here. Are you interested?"

His deep chuckle was music to her ears. "When do I start?"

They spent the rest of the afternoon driving around the ranch, assessing what needed to be done. Millie had been right; all of the pastures were bone dry. It didn't take long to get the water started. All of the pastures were flood irrigated, so there wasn't much to it. Most of the work wasn't hard; it just needed to be done at the right time.

Teal felt better about things by the time they walked back to the house. Nick had known exactly what needed to be done and already had a plan for it. "The first thing we'll do tomorrow is move the herd to another pasture. They're overgrazing the one they're on."

"We can keep moving them north until we get everything irrigated," Teal agreed. By this time they had reached the back door and could see Millie moving around in the kitchen. "Come on in, Nick, and I'll introduce you to Millie."

Millie turned at the sound of their voices. "How did things go today, Teal?" There was an anxious look on her face, and worry sounded in her voice.

"Well, first let me introduce you to Nick Marcus. He's going to be our ranch foreman from now on. Nick, this is Millie Carpenter."

Nick stepped past Teal to grasp Millie's hand. "Nice to meet you, ma'am."

"It's nice to meet you too, Nick." She turned questioning eyes to Teal. "Are you going to explain this to me?"

"I will if you promise to feed us. I'm starving."

Nick rolled his eyes. "She ate a horse for lunch; I don't know how she could possibly be starving."

"I missed breakfast," Teal defended herself as she walked to the refrigerator to pour a glass of milk.

The camaraderie between them was amazing to Millie. But all she said was, "Both of you sit down. I have dinner all ready."

While they ate roast beef and mashed potatoes, Teal told Millie the events of the day. She made sure to gloss over the horror of the attack; Millie certainly didn't need to hear the gory details. "So, that's about it," she finished. "We'll have to move Joe's things out of the trailer, so Nick can move in."

"The trailer doesn't belong to Joe?" Nick asked, breaking into Teal's account of the day.

"I guess I've gotten used to calling it Joe's trailer, but it belongs to my dad's estate. It'll be staying right here. I just hope it won't be too much of a problem to move Joe out.''

''You should let him do it himself, or else have a witness on hand. He might break all his things and then claim that you did it and sue you for it.'' Nick certainly wouldn't put it past the man to try. He was obviously extremely bitter.

Teal chewed her lip thoughtfully. ''Well, I guess you'll have to sleep here until he's gone then. Which room do you think would be best, Millie?''

''I'll make up the room down here as soon as I clean up this kitchen. Why don't you two go on into the living room and relax. You deserve it after the day you had, girl.''

Nick followed Teal through the dining room and into the living room. The dark paneling on the walls and the heavy oak furniture seemed totally masculine and completely at odds with Teal's lively personality. Teal noticed his scrutiny and explained, ''My father had this room redone after I left for college. If he were here, you'd see how perfectly it fit him. Sometimes I feel like he's with me when I sit here in the dark. His presence lives in this room. I don't think I could possibly bear to change it.''

''It's good to have places like that,'' Nick agreed. ''It somehow makes it easier to part with a loved one.''

They sat down at opposite ends of the couch while Teal commented, "You sound like you've lost someone before."

The couch was deep and soft and Nick took a moment to settle in before responding. "Yes. My mother."

"I'm sorry."

"It was quite a while ago."

A silence of remembrance fell as they both thought about the ones they'd lost. Nick was the first to recover; he mentally shook himself and tried to brighten the mood. The last thing Teal needed was talk of sad things after the horrendous day she'd had. "You said you'd been to college. Where did you go?"

"Oh . . . um, I went to UNC in Greeley." The change in topic threw her for a moment.

"Tell me about it. What did you study?"

"Oh, it's a boring story. You don't want to hear it."

"Of course I do. I wouldn't have asked if I didn't."

"All right, you asked for it," Teal said with a small smile. "I got a B.A. in physical education. I really loved all of my courses, learning about the body and how it works. I especially liked the first aid courses and athletic training that I took. It really made a difference when I started coaching. My athletes were always complaining of some ailment or other. I was an assistant volleyball and basketball coach my last two years of college and then I got a job at one of the high schools in Greeley and I took over the head coaching position in volleyball. I really enjoyed working with those kids, but I have to admit that teaching P.E. in Greeley wasn't what I'd expected. I guess it was because I went to a small school up here in Walden. Everyone knew everybody else. It felt like a real community, but Greeley was too big. Actually it's considered a small town, but still there were drugs and weapons and all kinds of problems. And the politics involved in teaching was unreal. Incompetence was overlooked just because of the good-old-boy network. I admit that I hated that part. So, when my position was cut due to lack of funds, it was pretty easy to leave it all behind.''

''Sounds like you are quite an athlete, teaching P.E. and coaching sports.''

''Yeah, I guess you could say that. I've always liked to be outdoors, and I hate to just sit around. I guess sports were the logical outlet. What about you? Do you like sports?''

''I played football in high school—quarterback. I had a pretty good arm until I injured my shoulder and had to quit. If I hadn't been injured my life would probably be a lot different. I would have gone to college on an athletic scholarship and gotten a job. But, as it turned out, I was more interested in ranching. My father was more than happy to have me stay home and help him.'' Nick shrugged with regret. "Now I'm learning from other people and from different experiences. When I've seen enough I'll look for a place of my own.''

"You certainly have a lot of enthusiasm for Colorado. Do you think you'll stay here?''

"I do like it up here, but I don't really know yet where I want to settle. For now I'm enjoying traveling around. I'm only twenty-seven; there's still plenty of time to settle down.''

Teal felt an easy camaraderie with him that she rarely experienced with anyone. She felt like she'd known him for years, when in fact she had met him only a short while ago. Something about him made it easy for her to confide in him. With some effort she forced her mind back to the conversation. "It's funny," she mused, "but once I turned twenty-one I didn't really feel the need to have any more birthdays. Already I'm twenty-five—a third of my life is gone. Somehow, I never thought of myself as getting old. Ironic, isn't it?''

Nick burst out laughing. "Remind me to get you a cane and a rocking chair."

Teal laughed along with him, seeing the humor in what she'd just said. "But I really mean it. Can you picture yourself getting old?"

He grimaced at the thought. "I try not to."

Teal laughed again at his expression. "I think I could see you with gray hair and a cane, rocking away on your front porch."

"Oh, now I'm the one with a rocking chair. Don't get that picture too firmly in your mind. I'm going out of this life riding a horse across my own land. No rocking chair for me."

In her mind's eye she could actually see him doing just that. She wondered what it would be like to grow old with him. Immediately she started. Where had that thought come from? The last thing she needed was a relationship with Nick. She needed him too much to help her run the ranch. A relationship would just complicate things. Best get any thought like that out of her head. Right now she needed to focus all of her energy on getting the ranch back into shape.

With that thought in mind, Teal spent the next hour going over with Nick everything that needed to be done and discussing his salary. He seemed happy with the figure they settled on and immediately launched into some of the great ideas he had that were going to save them lots of time in the long run. Teal found herself looking forward to all the work ahead of them; his enthusiasm was catching.

"Well, I guess that about covers it," Teal concluded with a yawn.

"You've had an awfully long day. The best thing for you is a good night's rest. Why don't you sleep in tomorrow morning and I'll get things started by myself."

Teal was touched by the offer. She'd never known anyone to be so solicitous before. "I appreciate the offer Nick, but I'm perfectly fine. I think I will turn in, though. Would you like me to show you to your room before I do?"

"Sure."

Teal led the way through the dining room and down the hall to the back of the house. Once she'd turned the light on in Nick's room it was obvious that Millie had already made up the bed and dusted the furniture. The bedspread was turned down, making the bed look soft and inviting. A wave of exhaustion swept over Teal just looking at it. "Will this be all right?" she asked.

Nick stepped by her and into the room; looking at the bed made him realize how tired he was, too. "It's just perfect, thank you."

"Okay, I'll see you in the morning then."

"Goodnight," Nick softly replied as he closed the door behind her.

Again the day dawned beautifully clear, and Nick and Teal made the most of the cool morning hours. After breakfast they saddled up two horses and headed out to move the herd to the next pasture. The creak of leather and the jingle of spurs mixed with the gentle lowing of the cows as they swished their way through the early morning dew sprinkled on the grass. Teal sighed with pleasure. This had been her favorite job when she was growing up. How had she ever thought that teaching school could compare to this? This was definitely where she belonged.

Her horse moved eagerly around the willows looking for any stray cows or calves that had gotten separated from the herd. The feel of the horse beneath her and the sun on her face began to renew her faith in herself. She certainly wouldn't admit it to anyone, but the attack had left her badly shaken. She'd had several nightmares during the night, making her realize just how much she appreciated the daylight and a chance to put the ranch back together with Nick's help. She was going to stick with this if it killed her; she wouldn't allow Joe or the memory of the attack to get the best of her. She knew that her father would be proud of the effort she was making—now all she had to do was make it work. She could almost feel her father beside her conveying a feeling of contentment. She was doing the right thing. She smiled at the thought and a part of her that had been grieving for him began to heal.

"How's it going?" Nick asked as they met again by the gate.

Teal grinned widely. "I think we got them all."

"You look like the cat that ate the canary. What are you so all fired up about?"

"Oh, it just feels so good to be on a horse again. You know, I really love this ranch." It was easy, in the light of day, to forget about the dreams. She was going to do her best to focus on the positive things in her life; worrying certainly wasn't going to get her anywhere. At least with Nick she had something positive to look at.

Nick smiled at her excitement. He was glad to see her looking so optimistic. He had been afraid that the attack would seriously bother her, especially while she was dealing with losing her father. "I know what you mean. There's nothing better than going for a ride first thing in the morning, especially in beautiful country like this."

Teal was feeling too energetic to sit around talking. Now that they had the cattle moved she was feeling as frisky as her horse. "Wanna race?"

"That depends."

"On what?"

"What do I get if I win?"

Teal chuckled softly. "What makes you think you're going to win?"

"Okay, what do I have to give up if I lose?"

"I'll let you name the price."

Nick rubbed his jaw absently as he thought of something to wager with. He smiled as he came up with a no-lose situation for himself. "If I win, you have to take me out to dinner in town. If you win, I have to take you to dinner anywhere you want to go." Either way he was a winner; spending time with her was certainly a perk of the job.

Teal burst out laughing. "You got it. First one to the hill across the pasture is the winner. Are you ready?"

Nick nodded with an evil grin. The horses sensed their excitement and began to prance and throw their heads.

"Go!" Teal yelled as she spurred her horse into a gallop. Nick's horse leaped beside her and they were off. Teal rode low over her horse's neck and urged him on while the thrill of the competition sang in her veins. Nick watched her as they raced across the pasture, thrilling at the sight of her hair whipping in the wind. They charged up the hill dead even and reined in their horses. Exhilaration danced in their eyes as they laughed together.

Teal was the first to catch her breath. "I guess you'd call that a tie."

"I guess so."

"What does that do to our wager?"

"We're going dutch."

They both laughed at that. "I'll get you next time," Teal warned.

"Wanna bet?"

They laughed again and Teal couldn't remember the last time she'd had so much fun. This man had walked into her life and in one day he'd turned it completely around. It was incredible. She found herself cherishing every moment they spent together. Work had never been so entertaining before.

The day passed quickly as they worked their way from chore to chore. There was an overwhelming amount of work to be done, but it didn't seem so bad. They were taking one thing at a time, and their camaraderie made the time fly by. It had been dark for hours by the time they made it back to the house for dinner.

Teal's mouth watered at the smell of fried

chicken wafting out the back door. "Millie, that smells heavenly," she stated as she walked in the door. "I hope it's ready to eat."

"Don't tell me—you're starving," Millie finished for her.

"How'd you guess?"

"I'm beginning to get the drift here," Nick put in. "She guessed because you're always starving. Isn't that right Millie?"

"You got it," Millie answered with a grin.

Teal took the teasing good-naturedly. "I've got a right to be hungry. I've been working my fingers to the bone all day."

"Here, let me see," Nick said as he grasped one of her hands and studied her fingers. "Nope, no bone there that I can see. I think she definitely needs short rations," he said as he smiled toward Millie.

"We'll give her whatever the two of us don't eat," Millie agreed.

A shock wave of feeling rioted up Teal's arm at Nick's touch. She was glad that he was looking at Millie and didn't see the surprise on her face. His hands were rough from all the work he did, in sharp contrast to the gentleness of his touch. She'd never experienced anything like it, and she was reluctant to remove her hand from his.

She covered her reaction by playing along with

the two of them. "Millie! I'm shocked. This man has been here for only a day and already he's won you over to his side. You know we women are supposed to stick together."

"Oh, all right. I guess there's enough here for you too."

"I'm ever so grateful," Teal answered with a theatrical bow to them both. Nick continued to hold on to her hand. Somehow it felt completely right to leave it there.

Nick gave her hand a squeeze before he let go. "I guess you held up your end of the work today. Millie and I will be sure to let you gnaw on our chicken bones as a reward."

"Are you going to pat me on the head like a good little doggie while you're at it?"

"Only if you're really good," Nick answered as he sat down at the table.

"You better watch out," Teal warned as she sat across from him. "Sometimes animals turn on their owners."

"Never bite the hand that feeds you," Nick admonished with a shake of his finger in her direction.

Millie burst out laughing at the two of them. "I've never known that girl to bite me before. Why don't you two hush up and eat?"

Nick grinned across at her as he filled his plate

with chicken and dumplings. Teal returned the grin and contentedly began to eat. Millie shook her head as she watched the two of them. She'd never seen two people take to each other the way these two had. It did her heart good to see it. Teal needed someone like Nick to help her get back on her feet. Millie sighed with pleasure at the thought as she too began to eat.

"How long do you expect to be staying in this area, Nick?" Millie asked curiously.

"I don't know exactly. I imagine I'll stay for at least a year, if that works out all right with Teal. I always like to stay at least that long to get a feel for all the seasons and experience the differences in work due to the weather." He glanced at Teal for her reaction.

She tried to keep her face from showing her disappointment. She had hoped that he would want to stay here indefinitely—even make the place his home. Well, at least she had a year to convince him to stay. "The longer you can stay, the better," she assured him. "There'll always be plenty of work to do around here."

"What do you plan to do after that?" Millie asked.

"I'm just traveling around, seeing the country. I imagine I'll find another ranch to work on somewhere."

"Sounds lonely," Millie commented gruffly.

"Oh, I guess it can be at times. I guess I'm looking for a place to call home. When I find it I'll settle down and buy my own land. Until then I'm just enjoying myself."

"Is that why you stay for a year? Check out all the seasons in case you want to stay?" Teal asked. She held her breath as she waited for his answer. If it was yes, she had a better chance of keeping him on. He'd already said how much he liked the mountains.

"Yeah, that's one of the reasons. Experience is another and being fair to my employer is a good one, too."

"That makes sense," Teal agreed. "Well, I hope the mountains work their magic on you and persuade you to stay. I've already gotten used to you being here."

"What kind of magic are the mountains supposed to work on a person?" Nick asked.

"That's just what I call it," Teal explained. "I've never been able to leave Colorado for very long at a time. They just seem to call to me; no place else can compare. Oh, I know there are some beautiful places to see, but the mountains have a mystical beauty of their own. I can't explain it, but I've heard other people say the same thing. Once they've lived in the mountains, no place else will do. It's magical,'' she said with an other-wordly lilt to her voice.

Nick shook his head in disbelief. ''And do you agree with her, Millie?''

''I certainly do,'' she proclaimed. ''I grew up in Kansas, but I'd never go back. Don't get me wrong—life in the mountains can be extremely difficult, even dangerous at times, but there's nothing else like it. You'll see.''

''Maybe it's the danger that's addicting,'' Teal offered.

''What kind of danger are we talking about?'' Nick asked. He was willing to go along with their story, but he didn't believe a word of it. They were just telling him a tall tale to pull his leg.

''Well, like the weather for instance. We've known winter storms that have shut us in for days. And there's always the wild animals. They get to prowling around a lot more in the spring when they're good and hungry. I've seen quite a few bears over the years. Basically, you just can't take anything for granted up here the way you can down in a city. You always have to be on your toes and that makes you feel more alive. Does that help?'' Teal asked. She desperately wanted him to fall in love with this area the way she had. She couldn't even think of him leaving. Already it felt right to have him there. It was too soon to analyze why it was so important; all she cared about was keeping him there.

"That part I can believe. There are those same dangers in other parts of the country also. And I certainly see your point about the great outdoors; living in the city would be awful in comparison. But I think I'll reserve judgment on the mountain magic part." His skepticism was obvious from his expression.

Millie and Teal smiled at each other knowingly.

Chapter Three

June slowly wound its way through July and into August, and gradually they began to catch up on all the work that had to be done before winter set in. They had been working ten to fourteen hours every day, and their effort was finally paying off. Joe had moved his things out of the trailer, but it would still be quite some time before he went to trial. The case was on the docket for the middle of next year, and until then Joe was out on bail. He was restrained from going anywhere near Teal and from leaving the state; other than that, he was a free man.

Teal didn't have time to worry about it, and eventually the horror of the attack lessened and her bad dreams abated. It took a lot of effort, but at last she and Nick were getting the ranch back into shape. She was finally beginning to feel like she truly belonged. The work was satisfying and the exercise left her pleasantly tired, making it easier to fall asleep and stay that way each night. She mourned the loss of her father every day, but working on the ranch he had loved so much somehow made it easier to deal with. She was preserving her father's way of life, and that made her feel good inside.

Nick was also a big part of her healing process. She'd never laughed so much in her entire life. Every minute with him was a joy; she'd begun to look at her life from a different angle and Nick had made all that possible. She didn't realize how important he was becoming to her until it snuck up on her and slapped her in the face.

The first Sunday in August dawned clear and slightly cool. Teal stretched lazily in her bed before rising. It felt so good just to lie there. Every Sunday when she was growing up her father would take her down to the river and teach her how to fish. She smiled to herself as she remembered the feel of a frisky trout biting at the end of her line. She really missed that.

She sat up sharply as an idea began to take hold. "Why not?" she exclaimed. She giggled to herself as she hurriedly threw on some clothes and practically ran down the stairs.

Millie heard her coming and turned from the

stove to look at her in surprise. ''Where's the fire this morning, girl?''

''I just had the greatest idea Millie, but I need your help.'' Teal's eyes were bright with excitement and her face was flushed from her rush down the stairs. ''Will you help me?''

''I will if I can. What kind of idea are you talking about?''

''I think Nick and I are caught up enough to take a day off and go fishing. You remember—dad and I did that every Sunday.'' Millie nodded and Teal rushed on. ''I need you to help convince Nick to go with me. You know how he is—work, work, work. What do you say? Will you help me?''

Millie hadn't seen Teal this excited in years. It made her happy to see her coping with everything so well. Of course she'd help convince Nick. The girl deserved a day off. ''I'll do you one better—I'll even pack a picnic lunch so you can make a day of it. Both of you have been working way too hard. It'll do you good to relax for a while.''

Teal squealed and hugged Millie exuberantly. ''Thanks Millie; you're the greatest.''

They were startled when Nick opened the back door. He walked in and smiled at them both. ''Am I interrupting something?''

Teal made up a story to distract him. ''No, not

at all,'' she gushed. ''Millie was just telling me some great news about her family, that's all.''

She should have known that he wouldn't just leave it at that. His eyes lighted up and he smiled at Millie. ''Does your family live in Kansas? I know you said you'd lived there.''

''My brother still does,'' Millie admitted. ''My niece just got accepted to Harvard.''

Teal almost admonished Millie for not telling her, but she managed to clamp down on her tongue in time. ''Isn't that great news, Nick?'' she said instead.

''It is.'' He smiled with admiration at Millie. ''What's she going to study?''

''Law. I can hardly believe that one of my family is going to be a lawyer.''

''That's great, Millie. Congratulations.''

''Oh, don't congratulate me, Nick. I didn't have anything to do with it, but I'm sure happy for that girl. She always was a go-getter. Now, what can I fix you for breakfast?''

''Whatever's easiest,'' Nick answered as he always did. He knew how hard Millie worked and he certainly didn't want to make it any more difficult for her. Besides that, he could eat just about anything and be happy.

''I'll just have a bowl of cereal this morning,'' Teal said as she sat down at the table.

"What's the matter?" Nick asked with concern. "Aren't you feeling well this morning?"

"Oh, just a little tired," she answered, doing her best to hide her smile. She had him right where she wanted him now.

Millie was quick to catch on. "You certainly have been working awfully hard. And you know you haven't taken a day off since Nick started working here. I would think that the two of you would be caught up enough to take the day off and relax for awhile."

"I guess we are pretty much caught up, now that you mention it, Millie," Teal said.

Nick was really worried. He'd never seen Teal act like she was tired before. She toiled beside him every day and never once looked like she'd had enough. Most of the time he kept going so that she wouldn't know how tired he was. It would look bad if his employer had more energy than he did. She had probably been pushing herself too hard and was coming down with something because of it. He should have been more sensitive to her. She was probably just using work to cover up the pain of losing her father and maybe even some leftover stress from the attack. He should have realized it and forced her to slow down. "We could slow down for a day. In fact, why don't you take the day off. I can service the equipment by myself. It won't take much to get it ready to start mowing the hay. You take a rest.''

Teal frowned. He had taken the bait, but she'd caught the wrong fish. "I'd feel way too guilty making you work while I lounge around. No, if you're going to work then so will I. Maybe I just need to eat something to get my energy going this morning."

"That's not necessary," Nick argued.

Before he could say any more, Millie interrupted. "You both look like you could use some relaxation. Besides, I have this terrible hankering for some fresh trout for dinner." She slyly shifted her gaze to Teal. "Why, I remember when you and your daddy used to bring in the best trout, twenty to twenty-two inches if they were an inch. My mouth's just watering with the thought. You two always had to make a competition of it if I remember correctly. Who used to win those bets?"

"I think we both had our share of victories," Teal answered. "I wonder if there are still some twenty inchers out there."

"You can catch twenty-inch trout on this river?" Nick asked.

"You're more likely to do that in the spring when the river is higher," Teal explained. "But I bet we could catch some good-sized ones for dinner. I mean, it's the least we could do for Millie."

"Don't you fish, Millie?" he asked.

"Now I don't mind a good fish once it's cleaned and boned, but don't you expect me to go down there and throw a hook in the water. A woman's got to have limits, you know."

Nick looked abashed. "I didn't mean that, Millie," he protested. "It just didn't seem fair to me that the two of us take off to have some fun while you stay here in the house and work. If you liked to fish, you could come with us."

"Now don't you worry about me. Once I clean up this kitchen and pack the two of you something for lunch, I'll be done for the rest of the day. I might just go visiting this afternoon, but I'll be sure to be back in time to fix those fish. Why, I might even buy a bottle of wine to go with it while I'm in town. How does that sound?"

It was all Teal could do to keep from laughing out loud. She and Millie had played him perfectly. Hot dog! "Millie, you're an angel," she said as she walked around the table and gave her a big hug. "Fishing sounds like the perfect way to spend the day. Dad always said it was the best way to get rejuvenated."

It didn't take long for Millie to pack them a picnic lunch while they raided the basement for fishing gear. First they slathered themselves with mosquito repellent. The pesky insects were horrible in the middle of summer, making repellent a constant necessity. In no time at all they were down at the river at the first hole on Teal's property. Teal baited up with a lure while Nick opted for a spinner. Teal's lure looked just like a miniature trout, and Nick's spinner was silver with red spots that spun as he reeled in and also looked like live bait. They took turns throwing out into the deep hole and reeling in with the flow of the current. The rhythm of throwing out and reeling in came back like it had been mere days since Teal had been fishing. The gurgle of the river relaxed her and slowly she felt herself beginning to unwind.

"Are you getting any bites?" she asked.

"Not a one. Which reminds me—if we're going to be fishing for our dinner, we need to put a little wager on this event. How about double or nothing for that dinner in town that we haven't taken yet."

"You mean since we tied last time, we need to try again?"

"Exactly. If I catch the biggest fish, dinner's on you."

"Sounds good. Except let's get this perfectly clear so we don't argue later. What's the biggest fish to you? Are we talking longest or heaviest?"

"Longest."

"You're on."

They slowly meandered their way downstream,

fishing each hole that was formed by the bends and twists in the flow of the river. At about the middle of the ranch they came to the best spot on the river. The hole was too deep to see into and quite long and wide. Teal sat down on the grassy bank and lazily threw out her line. The only sounds she could hear were the lap of the water and the snap of their lines as they threw out and reeled in. They were the sounds of years ago when she used to come out here with her father. She sighed at the thought that she would never be able to do this with him again.

Nick sensed what that sigh meant. After what Millie had said earlier, she had to be reminiscing about Paul. ''I bet you and your father used to have a lot of good times down here.''

Teal looked up, startled. How did he always know what she was thinking about? It was uncanny. ''Yes, we did,'' she admitted. ''You know, I haven't fished in years. Actually, it's kind of nice to be carrying on this tradition. I think he'd want me to.''

''I imagine he'd just want you to be happy. Are you?''

Teal took a moment to think about it as she threw her line out yet again. ''I'm happy to be back on the ranch. Being away from it certainly helped me to see how much I appreciate the beauty up here.

And I'm very glad that Joe is gone and that you're here. I guess I haven't told you how much your help has meant to me. I could never have gotten this far without you.'' This was the first time she had ever said anything remotely serious to him. Usually they joked around and kept things light, but somehow she knew that she could say that to him, and that he would understand.

Nick was touched by her sincerity. ''Don't give me too much credit. You've certainly been pulling your end of the wagon.'' He paused for a second as he cast out his line. ''I'm really enjoying working here. I really love it up here—maybe there is something to that mountain magic after all.''

Teal laughed at his tone of voice. ''Oh, I know how skeptical you are about that. You just wait. It'll hit you sooner or later.''

''Most likely later,'' he replied with a hint of sarcasm.

Teal laughed and gave herself up to just enjoying the time spent with him and the beauty of the morning. She wondered what would bring a man like him all the way out here. She knew the story he had told her, but surely there was more to it than that. On impulse, she scooted to a better angle so she could watch him as she fished. The phrase ''poetry in motion'' fit him perfectly as he cast his line with fluidity and grace. She knew how strong he was from the heavy lifting he'd done around the ranch, and it was intriguing to watch him control that strength with such finesse.

Her thoughts continued to wander, and soon she was wondering how the touch of those hands would feel to her, if he were to turn toward her and see her as a woman rather than just his boss. Her skin tingled at the idea. His hair looked so soft lying across the collar of the hooded sweatshirt he was wearing—her fingers itched to glide through it. She could even imagine how soft his chocolate brown eyes would look, gazing into hers just before he kissed her.

She was startled out of her daydream by a big bite on the end of her line. She shifted her attention back to the river as she continued to reel slowly. A sharp tug hit the end of her line again, and then continued to pull. With a jerk of her pole she set the hook and began to bring in the fish. She could tell he was a big one by the way he was fighting her.

Nick dropped his pole and stood up behind her to get a better look. ''Boy, that must be a big one. Now don't let him get away,'' he admonished.

''Don't try that head game with me,'' she said as she continued to play the fish closer and closer to the bank. ''You are not going to make me nervous enough to lose this fish. He's all mine.''

"Who me? I would never do something like that. Maybe you should pull a little bit harder."

"Why? So he can break my line?"

"Now don't get a negative attitude. He might just get away from you."

Teal ignored him as she finally pulled the trout onto the bank. He was a beauty. She smiled up into Nick's eyes as he bent over her. "Ha! Beat that."

"What, that little thing? You must be joking."

"Little! Get your tape measure. Let's make this official."

Nick retrieved the tape measure from his creel and stretched it across the squirming trout. It extended all the way out to eighteen inches. "Eighteen isn't bad, but it's not twenty either," he declared.

"Doesn't have to be, if you don't catch anything bigger."

He continued to loom over her as she placed the trout into her creel. Her hands began to shake as she thought about how close he was to her. They'd been working closely together for over a month, but suddenly her fantasy about him changed everything. He'd been affecting her all along, but up until now she had always been able to ignore it. Now she was seeing him in a whole new light, and her awareness of him was heightened to a fever pitch.

She didn't have anything left to do with her hands, so she sat back on her heels and looked up. He was bending over her with his hands on his thighs, watching every move she made. "Wha . . . what are you doing?" she asked nervously.

"Watching you," he answered quietly.

"Why?"

"Why were you watching me before you caught that fish?"

She blushed a bright pink as she held his eyes. How had he known that she was looking at him? She had been sitting mostly behind him, and he had never once turned his head to look at her. He continued to stand over her, waiting for an answer. "I, um . . . well, um . . . I was just studying your fishing technique. I wanted to make sure you weren't cheating or anything."

He smiled with a devilish look that told her he didn't believe a word of it. He had felt her looking at him—his skin had fairly tingled from her gaze. He hadn't expected her ever to look at him like that, but it certainly wasn't unpleasant. In fact, he had forgotten all about fishing.

Now he was looking at her as a woman rather than his boss, and she didn't know what to do. Her mind told her this was a bad idea, but her body refused to move away from him. "So, what's *your* excuse?" she asked in a breathless voice. Her heart was beginning to pound so hard she was sure he could hear it.

He reached out and twirled an end of her hair around his index finger. "I was wondering if your hair is as soft as it looks."

He really could read her mind!

"Is it?"

"Better." He dropped down onto one knee, bringing his face inches from her own. His eyes turned into the soft look that she had imagined as he whispered, "Are your lips just as soft?"

Her heart threatened to pound right out of her chest as she responded, "There's only one way to find out."

He smiled sensually as his gaze dropped to her mouth. He leaned forward and touched his lips to hers, denying himself any other contact with her. The effect was explosive. Teal felt like her very bones were melting as her lips softened under his. A fire ignited between them and Nick dug his fingers into her hair to hold her still as he explored the sweetness she was offering him.

She grasped the front of his sweatshirt to hold him to her as she began to sway from the force of their passion. He pushed forward and she fell back onto the grass, pulling him with her. Teal lost all sense of time under the onslaught of feeling rocketing through her. She had been kissed before, but nothing had ever prepared her for this. She had always been so caught up in getting her degree and then in furthering her career that she had never had much time for the men in her life. No one had even begun to affect her—until now.

It was too much too soon, and they both seemed to realize it at the same time. Nick drew back and she let go of his shirt. He had such a look of surprise on his face that she would have laughed except she knew that her own face looked just as shocked. They stared at each other without saying a word as they slowly caught their breath. Their relationship up until now had always been light and carefree. They had hit it off instantly, and it was obvious now that their banter had only been a cover for the passion waiting to erupt between them. Neither one of them had been ready for it before, and Teal still didn't feel like she was prepared for it now. She rolled away from him and sat up, nervously running her fingers through her hair to smooth it back down. She had left it down this morning and now it felt like a total mess.

Nick could feel her withdrawing from him, and he knew he had to say something to ease the tension between them. Nothing in his life had ever prepared him for the reaction he had felt with Teal just now. Shock was tying his tongue in knots, and he couldn't think of a thing to say to save the situation. "Teal . . . I," he began, but she cut him off.

"You don't have to say anything, Nick. I understand. I think I'm going to fish on down a ways. Why don't you stay here; there's still a lot of fish left in this hole. I'll meet you back at the house."

"What exactly is it that you understand, Teal? Somehow I don't think we're on the same wavelength anymore." Her total withdrawal cut him to the quick. How could she just get up and walk away after what they had just shared?

She didn't answer him or turn to look back as she walked away. In seconds the willows swallowed her up and he couldn't even see her anymore. Every muscle in his body screamed to follow her, but he knew that this wasn't the time. She needed to be alone right now. It might even give him time enough to think of something to say.

Chapter Four

Nick walked slowly back to the yard. Fishing was no longer appealing and he figured that working on machinery would be a good outlet for his frustration. He always found something to work on when he was upset, and the equipment needed to be serviced before they got the hay in. They were already behind in cutting it as it was. Since Joe hadn't irrigated the pastures when they'd needed it they'd had to keep the water running longer than normal, and the grass was just now ready to be cut. They were really cutting the pasture grass to feed to the herd for winter, but everyone in the mountains called it "hay". It would be cut and then baled into huge round rolls that could be hoisted onto a truck and fed a bit at a time through the winter.

Teal heard him banging away in the yard when she walked in later that evening. She had fished all day until she had finally caught four fish. The

river was low this late in the year, making it difficult to catch anything. They were all pretty good-
sized, which was sure to please Millie and her
dinner plans. Teal wasn't in the least bit hungry,
and the thought of sitting across from Nick and
making polite conversation was daunting, to say
the least.

She had reacted badly that morning and she
knew it. Nothing had prepared her for something
like that, though that wasn't much of an excuse.
Nick had every right to be angry with her. Or hurt.
At first, she had run away because she was afraid
of letting herself feel too much emotion. Her father
and Millie were the only people who had ever been
important to her, and she had already lost one of
them. What if she lost Nick, too? After a couple
of hours she had realized that that was a terrible
way to look at life. Running away from love would
never solve anything.

Once she had come to terms with that, however,
another problem struck her. She needed Nick's
help to make it through the winter. Some of the
hardest work on the ranch was in wintertime. What
if something went wrong with their relationship—
if they even decided to have one? Obviously they
wouldn't be capable of working together anymore.
She had seen enough relationships go sour, and
none of the women she knew were ever able to

remain "just friends" with an ex-boyfriend. She had to think of the ranch first. After this winter she would probably be able to take care of everything by herself. But for now she needed experienced help. Somehow she had to make Nick understand that.

Millie had seen Nick working in the yard when she had come home that afternoon. The look on Teal's face when she walked in the door confirmed her fears. Something had gone wrong. "Was the river too low for fishing?" she asked softly. If she gave her enough room, Teal would tell her what was wrong in her own good time.

"It wasn't too bad. I caught four." She pulled them out of her creel and placed them in the sink. "I cleaned them down at the river, but I'll wash them again."

"Don't worry about that. I'll get them ready for dinner. Why don't you go on up and take a nice hot bath. You look like you could use one."

"Thanks, Millie. That sounds heavenly." First she stored everything away in the basement, and then she ran upstairs to run a bath. The hot water was relaxing, and she let her mind float away as she soaked.

She felt much better when she returned to the kitchen for dinner. Nick was already seated and Millie was busy putting things on the table. Nick watched her enter with an unreadable expression; obviously he was waiting for her to make the first move. She didn't want to say anything in front of Millie, so she kept her first statement impersonal. "How does the machinery look? Is it going to make it through haying season?"

Nick didn't like the way she wouldn't quite meet his eyes. She was looking more at the bridge of his nose or the top of his forehead. But he was willing to wait if she was. "The equipment's old, but it's still in good condition. Either Paul or Joe took pretty good care of it. If it doesn't rain, I'll get started in the morning."

Millie frowned at the two of them. This was the first time she had ever heard either of them speak in such stilted voices. All traces of their camaraderie were gone. The trout was excellent, but the strain at the table kept all three of them from enjoying it. Even the wine they were drinking with dinner didn't loosen them up.

"Thanks for dinner, Millie. It was excellent as always. Goodnight," Nick said as he rose to leave.

Teal watched him walk out the door before she realized the implication. He was angry, and she definitely needed to explain things to him tonight. That thought galvanized her into action and she followed him outside.

"Wait, Nick," she called after him.

He stopped at the sound of her voice, but he didn't turn around.

"I'd like to talk to you, if you have a minute," Teal explained.

"All right."

He certainly wasn't making it easy for her, but she didn't really blame him. "I was rude to you this afternoon, and I apologize. I don't really have a very good excuse, except that I was scared. You certainly know how to kiss," she offered with a shaky laugh. If he would just turn around and look at her or say something she'd feel much better. She supposed she was expecting too much to have him laugh with her.

He did finally turn and look at her, but she couldn't see his eyes in the dark. He sighed heavily and put his hands in his back pockets as if he couldn't trust himself not to touch her. "What do you expect from me, Teal?" His frustration was clear, but he was wary, too.

"Well, I guess I hoped you'd accept my apology. And then maybe we could start over or something."

"Is that what you think we need? To start over?"

His attitude was starting to irritate her. The least he could do would be to meet her halfway. "I'm sorry, Nick. I don't have all the answers," she said angrily. "What do you suggest we do?"

"I suggest that you quit trying to pretend that there isn't something happening between us. It's as clear as the nose on your face. We can't just act like nothing happened today. It isn't going to go away." He lowered his voice before he continued, "I don't want it to go away."

Teal sucked her breath in sharply. His last words cascaded over her in a sensual flow that left her breathless. She was in trouble if his mere words could affect her like this. "I don't know what to do."

She looked so forlorn that it was all he could do to keep from gathering her into his arms. "What are you so afraid of?"

She took a deep breath before she answered. "I need to put this ranch before myself. Millie depends on me, and I admit that I don't know enough to keep it going by myself. I've seen a lot of relationships turn bad. If something were to go wrong between us, the business end of our relationship would suffer. You'd probably leave. Where does that leave me?"

Nick hadn't even begun to think along those lines, and her admission stunned him. "There aren't any guarantees in life, that's true. Living in fear of what might happen is also no way to live. There are risks in everything. Some people would look at it the other way—having a relationship with me might be more likely to keep me here.''

Teal didn't have an answer for that one. ''Maybe it was just too soon, or too much. I don't know. I haven't known you very long; I don't even know that much about you. Everything's going too fast.''

The pain in her voice finally touched him like nothing else could. He knew he was being too hard on her. He'd never known anyone like her, and he didn't want to waste a single minute of his time with her. But she was coming from a different place than he was; she'd just lost her father, and on top of that she was trying to adjust to a new way of life. For her, it was too much. ''Okay,'' he agreed.

''Okay? What does okay mean?''

''It means that I see your point. Maybe it is too fast for you. As long as you don't completely deny what is happening between us, I'm willing to take it slowly. As slow as you want.''

Teal sighed with relief. He didn't hate her. ''Can we just be friends for awhile? I feel like I need something steady, or maybe sturdy, to rely on for now. Is that asking too much?''

''There's more than just friendship between you and me, and you know it. But I'm willing to give you the time you need. I'm not going anywhere.''

For now they seemed to have called a truce, but

Teal wasn't sure she'd come out on the winning end as she lay uncomfortably in bed that night. Nick had been more than fair with her; at first she had been afraid he was going to pack up and leave. She knew that he wasn't the type of person to up and quit at the smallest provocation, but she relied so heavily on him that her fears got the best of her.

While her mind was trying to deal with her insecurities, her body was reminding her that it knew exactly what it wanted. The sheets and blankets on her bed were in a tangled mess, and she felt just as restless and uneasy as she had two hours ago when she had first climbed under the covers. It was almost like she had a deep itch beneath her skin that was impossible to scratch. Even though she knew that the cause of that itch was Nick, she couldn't just go to him to ease her discomfort. Her mind just wasn't ready.

Dark circles lined her eyes as she gazed at her reflection in the mirror the next morning. Her eyes were bloodshot and she couldn't think of another time she had looked as bad. She had slept now and then but had been awake most of the night, and her image reflected it. She sighed heavily in resignation and did her best to make herself look presentable.

Nick and Millie were already in the kitchen

when she walked in for breakfast. With one look at Nick the restlessness raging through her veins began to ease. Just being in the same room with him was soothing. Her mind wasn't strong enough this morning to deny how much of an effect he had on her.

"Good morning, Teal," Millie said. "What will you have for breakfast this morning?"

"Whatever you're having will be fine," she answered. She sat down across from Nick and noticed that his eyes were red and dark-rimmed too. A wave of tenderness washed over her at the sight. She knew that she should feel guilty for causing both of them a sleepless night, but for some reason all she felt was concern and sympathy for him. He had already told her he wanted to have a relationship with her, but the evidence of his sleepless night showed her how much he was affected by her. It did her heart good to see it.

He looked up as he felt her gaze on him. With one glance he could tell that she hadn't slept either, and immediately he felt better. He even managed to smile as he said, "Did you sleep well?"

She grinned as she lied, "Like a baby."

He cut her off before she could say any more. "A baby with colic?"

She couldn't help it; she had to laugh. The last

of the tension left her as he laughed along with her.

Millie sighed with relief at the sound. "Okay, you two—breakfast is ready." She set scrambled eggs, toast, and sausage down in front of them and watched as both of them heartily dug in. The tension of the evening before melted away, and this time all three of them enjoyed the meal.

When they were through, Teal followed Nick out of the house and across the yard. "What do you want me to do while you're cutting the hay?" she asked.

"Once I make sure everything is working correctly you can ride along with me and learn how to run the machine yourself. That's going to take me awhile though. Why don't you ride around the ranch and check the fences in the meantime. Make sure they're sturdy enough to withstand big drifts of snow. If you happen to find some spots that aren't strong enough, mark them and we'll fix them once the hay is cut."

"All right. I'll catch up with you later today then."

He nodded as she walked down the lane toward the barn. She needed the exercise, and it gave her a chance to think about Nick's reaction to her this morning. All traces of his anger and frustration were gone. Most men would probably have called

her a tease, but not Nick. She'd never known anyone so understanding and sensitive before. It would
be so nice to let go of her defenses and cuddle up
within the protective cocoon his caring would cre-
ate. The ranch came first, however, and she was
going to have to stick to her guns. Nick had said
that he was willing to wait—she had to be strong
enough to wait too.

Once she'd saddled a horse she felt better about
her decision as she rode around the ranch. This
land had been important to her father, and it was
just as important to her. She could build a lasting
friendship with Nick while they were running the
ranch, she reasoned. Only time would tell if there
was going to be something more between them.

She couldn't find any weak spots in the fence,
and she made it back to the yard by midafternoon.
Nick had a few acres of grass already cut and things
looked like they were going well. She grabbed a
quick bite to eat and then drove out to where Nick
was diligently working. She waited for him at the
end of the field and then climbed into the cab with
him.

"How are things going?" she asked loudly,
trying to make herself heard over the roar of the
engine.

"I had to adjust it some, but it seems to be
working perfectly for now." He began explaining

everything he was doing, and Teal listened avidly. After a few turns around the pasture she thought she had the basic idea and told him so.

"Okay," he agreed. "You try it."

He stopped and gave her his seat as he moved to sit beside her. She put it into gear and tried to remember all of his instructions. She'd never learned to cut the hay when her father was alive, and she couldn't believe how much she'd been missing. Something about it gave her a deep sense of satisfaction—working her own land was intoxicating. Now she knew why so many people were addicted to farming and ranching; there was a freedom to it that you couldn't get in any other job. She lost all track of time as she cut her way through acres of grass. She even forgot about Nick sitting patiently beside her watching her every move.

Nick knew that he had been forgotten, but he didn't care. Seeing her so enthralled with operating this big machine thrilled him, too. She had such a look of awe on her face that he couldn't look away from her. He'd always felt the same way about ranching, but he'd never seen that expression on anyone else's face before. She always managed to surprise him by doing the unexpected. He smiled to himself as he watched her; no matter how hard he looked he would never find another woman as enchanting as this one.

After a few hours he couldn't stand it anymore and interrupted her fascination. "Are you having fun?"

Teal jumped at the sound of his voice and turned her eyes toward him, startled. She had forgotten all about him sitting there. How embarrassing! She pushed in the clutch and brought the mower to a halt. "How long have you been sitting there?"

"You've been driving for a couple of hours. Don't worry about it; I could see how much fun you were having. I knew better than to interrupt, except now it's getting dark and I think the best hours for cutting are over. Why don't you just park it here by the road; that'll make it easier to get to in the morning. Once the dew goes off you can get started again."

"I can?"

"Obviously you're enjoying yourself, so why shouldn't you?"

"I don't know. I guess I haven't thought about it. Once I got started I forgot about everything else. Do you feel like I've been really wasting your time?"

"Not at all. I stayed out here with you just to make sure everything was going to keep operating right. There really isn't much else for you to do anyway, so I don't think it was a waste of time at all. In a couple of days I can start baling while you finish cutting. It'll go a lot faster that way."

Teal felt terribly awkward about just forgetting him like that. He'd been on her mind for the last twenty-four hours, and then when they were alone together she forgot about him. She figured that meant she had to be losing her mind. Ignoring it wasn't going to help; she had to say something about it. "I'm really sorry that I just forgot about you. That was a really rude thing to do, but I didn't do it intentionally. It's just that I've never driven anything like this before. I guess that's not a very good excuse, is it?"

"You don't have to explain it to me. I felt exactly the same way when my father first showed me how to drive a tractor, although I didn't forget that he was sitting next to me."

Teal blushed and looked away. She needed something to do with her hands so she shut off the motor and pulled out the key. Darkness was settling in and the stars were out in abundance. They both climbed down from the cab and Teal looked up at the sky, enjoying the vast expanse of the universe. Up in the mountains away from the lights of the town, the sky was much brighter, with many more stars.

"Can't find stars like that in the city, can you?" Nick asked, as he joined her in gazing at the sky.

''No, you sure can't,'' she agreed. ''I can find about four times more up here than I could when I lived in Greeley.''

''You're lucky to have a ranch like this.''

He sounded almost homesick and Teal wondered what had made him give up his life in Oklahoma. ''You sound like you miss your family's ranch. Have you been home lately?''

''Not since I left.'' He dismissed her question entirely, even though he knew what she was getting at. He just didn't want to talk about it. ''I'm going to find me a ranch like this some day.''

Teal accepted the switch in conversation. ''You mean in Colorado?''

''Yeah. I like it here.''

Was he trying to tell her something with those words? He knew that she wanted to rely on him— was this his way of reassuring her? She wished she knew.

''In fact,'' he went on, ''I haven't seen a ranch I like better anywhere. Have you ever thought about offering someone a partnership here?''

Teal sucked in her breath at that. ''What kind of partnership?''

''I guess that depends on what kind of partnership you're looking for.''

Guessing at what he meant was killing her. ''I feel like we're talking on two different levels, like we're having two conversations at once. Something tells me you're not just talking business.''

"Would it bother you if I weren't?"

Surely he wasn't talking about marriage, was he? "I think you need to spell out exactly what you mean.''

"Oh, you know what I mean. You let me know when you're ready to discuss it.''

With that he turned and walked to the pickup, leaving her staring after him dumbfounded.

They had so much work to do getting the hay cut and baled that Teal never got around to discussing what he meant. It was easier to let things coast along while they got the ranch back on an even keel. Their camaraderie had returned and they got along beautifully as long as Teal didn't think about what his closeness did to her. She managed through sheer force of will not to touch him or get too close to him, and so was able to survive their working relationship.

Nick carried on like he didn't have a care in the world. He never seemed to be bothered when she happened to be in close proximity to him. He kept everything light and just concentrated on getting the work done. It was almost like he'd totally forgotten their passionate interlude.

When Teal lay sweating and uncomfortable in her rumpled bed at night she cursed him for the torture he was putting her through. During the day she regained her equilibrium and knew that he was just obeying her wishes. She just wished he wouldn't do it so well. Some sign of discomfort on his part would help at least a little, but she never saw one.

That was just the way Nick wanted it. He kept iron control of himself all day, barely lasting until dark, when he could retreat to the trailer and fall apart in solitude. His bed was just as rumpled as hers when he got up in the morning, but Teal would never know that. It was the only satisfaction he could find.

Chapter Five

Eventually, the strain of pretending that Teal didn't matter to him became overwhelming and Nick knew that he needed a break. It had taken them until the end of September to get the ranch and the herd ready for winter, but they finally accomplished all that needed to be done. It had already snowed several times in September, and the weather was no longer warm. It was a relief to get away from the mosquitoes, but the cold made it difficult to work outdoors for very long. Nick was feeling pretty grouchy because of the weather and the pressure of pretending that Teal didn't affect him. October was deer-hunting season, and he began to make plans to get away by himself. He had always loved getting away from people and pitting himself against the elements. Hunting was just what he needed to rejuvenate himself before winter really set in.

Two days before rifle season opened Nick

alerted Teal to his plans. They were sitting at the dinner table that evening and had just finished eating a big meal. "Teal," he said calmly to get her attention.

The switch in the timbre of his voice had her immediately attentive. "Yes?"

"I just wanted to let you know that I'm going to take off for a few days. We're caught up on the work, and I need a break. Is that all right with you?"

Teal could feel the blood rushing out of her face, leaving her pale and ashen. She had been afraid he would leave. He'd said a few days—she had to make sure that's all it was. "Where would you go for just a few days?"

"Deer season opens the day after tomorrow. I think I'll backpack into some of that BLM land west of here and see what I can find. Is that a problem?" The Bureau of Land Management held public land, open to everyone, that made for good hunting.

Relief flooded Teal's system and a smile lit her face at the thought of hunting deer. "Dad used to take me hunting with him when I was a teenager. Do you remember, Millie?"

"I sure do. The thought of being that cold has always seemed ridiculous to me, but you would be so excited. It never seemed to bother you at all.

You came back just as excited as the day you left. Talking about how you'd learned to shoot and everything. Boy, those were the days.''

"You never told me you'd been hunting before," Nick said, a question in his voice.

"I guess that's because we've never talked about hunting before. You never said you liked to hunt either. How far are you going to go?"

"Not far. Maybe ten miles from here. I'll probably only be gone for two or three days. There's so much wildlife up here that I don't think it will take me long to bag my limit."

"How much is the limit nowadays?" Millie asked.

"Just one. They've really gotten tougher about their hunting and fishing limits in the last couple of years. Which reminds me, Millie, do you like to cook wild game or should I give the deer to a homeless shelter?"

"That's a good idea, Nick, giving it to a shelter," Millie agreed. "I could fix us a couple of steaks from it, and the rest could go to the needy. We certainly don't need the whole thing."

"Do you always go hunting by yourself?" Teal asked.

"No. When I was a kid my brothers and I always went with my father. We used to have some really good times. My mother was still alive then, and she loved to cook wild game. She thought it was a challenge to make it taste good. Whatever she did certainly worked, because it was delicious. I've done some duck hunting since I left home, but this will be the first time I've gone deer hunting by myself.''

''Would you like some company?'' Teal asked.

Nick sat back and pondered for a moment. This trip had been to get away from the strain of pretending with her, and now she wanted to come along. The thought of going camping with her was certainly appealing, but he knew he couldn't pretend to be disinterested any longer.

Teal could see that he wasn't thrilled by the idea. ''I wouldn't get in your way or anything. I'm very good at sitting motionless, and I cook a pretty mean camp meal.''

She looked so excited by the idea that he didn't have the heart to turn her down. Now wasn't the time to warn her of the consequences, but he would do that before they left. ''All right—you can come. I'll just give you fair warning that you have to pull your own weight.''

''No problem,'' she assured him.

A warm front had come through, melting the snow and leaving some grass for the herd to graze while she and Nick were gone. They hadn't started feeding them hay yet, and probably wouldn't have to for a while. The cows knew how to find grass even when it was under inches of snow; they'd be all right by themselves. The rest of the ranch work was taken care of, making it easy for them to leave for three days.

They were going to drive the pickup and a horse trailer as far as they could, and then ride and walk the rest of the way. They needed the horses to pack their gear and to bring the game back down when they had bagged their limit. Millie packed them plenty of food to eat, and they left the ranch at four-thirty in the morning.

Nick warned Teal before they got in the truck that morning. ''This isn't going to be a cake walk you know. It's cold at night, and mostly just hard work.''

''I know, Nick. I've gone before. I like this kind of thing. Don't worry about me.''

In a softer tone he added, ''It's just going to be you and me, you know.''

His tone of voice mixed with the implied message to hit her with a surprisingly sensual force. Her stomach clenched from the shock of it. Breathlessly, she answered again. ''Don't worry about me.''

Nick nodded his head. ''Well, let's go.''

It didn't take them long to drive as far as the

road would take them. They unloaded the horses in the frosty morning air and packed all of their gear onto the saddles. They had tents, sleeping bags, cooking utensils, food, and hunting equipment, which didn't leave much room for them to ride. It was a lot of weight for the horses to carry, but they weren't going far. They rode higher into the mountains for a couple of miles before finding a place to make camp. They made quick work of unsaddling the horses and hobbling them before they walked further uphill to find a good hunting spot.

They had dressed warmly in insulated coveralls with thick gloves and socks, but the air was cold and it slowly seeped in under their layers of protection. Even though they were hiking, Teal could feel her toes and fingers getting colder and colder. They stopped to rest after an hour of walking and their breath puffed out in big white clouds of steam. The orange vests they were wearing to make them stand out to other hunters were totally at odds with the quiet of the surrounding mountainside.

Eventually they found a spot to hide in while they waited for the deer to come to them. It was even colder sitting down, but just being with Nick in this wonderfully peaceful place was enough for Teal, and she didn't mind the numbness seeping into her bones.

They didn't have any luck that day and had to walk back to camp early in the afternoon to set things up before dark. They each had a tent and a five-pound down sleeping bag to keep them warm. Nick got a fire going, and they both huddled around it to thaw their fingers and toes.

Teal took a deep breath of fresh mountain air mixed with the woodsy smell of their fire. She loved being outdoors, surrounded by nature. It still amazed her to think that she might have missed this if her life hadn't been turned so completely around last summer. The orange flames of the fire popped and crackled and she smiled to herself at the sight. "Is there anything better than a fire?" she asked Nick.

"As long as it's not too dry around us it's wonderful. I'd hate to be the one that started a forest fire."

"Yes," she agreed. "You do have to be careful. It's not so pleasant to watch fire destroy property, but it certainly warms the heart to watch a small campfire like this one. It smells good, too."

"Hunting season has always been my favorite time of year. There's something about being cold that makes you appreciate your campfire even more."

"You said you've gone hunting with your family. Tell me about them." She'd been dying to know more about his family for months, and she had finally found the opportunity to ask about them.

"What do you want to know?"

"Well, I don't know. Just what they're like, things like that."

"My father is sixty years old now, and has been ranching almost all his life. He's built up his place out in Oklahoma to a really nice spread. Actually, he's pretty well known out there. He was hit pretty hard when my mother died, but he was recovering well when I left."

Teal was astonished at the bitterness in his voice as he mentioned his mother. She'd never seen him look or sound like that before. There was a lot there that he wasn't telling her.

He went on, and his tone lightened as he began to talk about his brothers. "My oldest brother, Dave, went to college at O.U. and learned a lot of things that my father was willing to incorporate into his operation. They get along real well, my father and Dave."

Teal interrupted. "Did Dave study ranching in college then?"

"I forget what the degree is called exactly, but yes, he learned everything he ever needed to know about ranching. Although I think he's learning more from my father than he did from college."

"Hands-on experience probably teaches you a lot more than books."

"I think so," Nick agreed. "I think of my traveling around for the last five years as my college education. The only difference is that I get paid instead of paying for tuition."

"You mentioned before that you have two brothers. Who's the other one?" she asked, trying to get him back on the subject of his family.

"He's three years older than me. Andrew is thirty, and Dave is thirty-four. Andrew went to college too, but he's more of the party animal type. I think he learned more about socializing than he did about anything else."

"He works with your father too, though, doesn't he?"

"Yep. It's a real family business all right." A slight hint of bitterness crept back into his tone with those words.

"A family business, but without you?"

"I know what you're getting at, but it's not worth the effort. Like I said before—I don't fit in with their way of thinking, and that's all there is to it."

"Don't you miss them at all?" She couldn't believe that he had a family that he wouldn't talk to at all. She'd give anything to have a sibling or two, and to have her father back would be heaven.

Surely, he couldn't just forget about them, as if they didn't exist.

"Sometimes, I guess. But it's better this way. Believe me."

"What if something happened to one of them? Wouldn't you regret all these years apart?"

Nick stared down into the flames and didn't answer. She'd just about given up hope that he was going to when he said, "I probably would."

"You'd regret it?"

"Yeah."

"Why don't you do something about it while you still have time? I bet they regret this break with you, too. You'll never know unless you try."

"It's not that simple."

"Maybe you're just making it too hard."

He stared at her with an unreadable expression. She held her breath for fear that he would get angry with her. She'd really gone too far, and she knew it. She'd didn't know anything about it—maybe he did come from one of those families that would disown you at the drop of a hat. Her heart skipped a beat at the thought. A man like Nick deserved a loving and close family. She wished she could do something to help.

"I'm sorry. I shouldn't have said that," she apologized.

"That's all right. You could be right."

* * *

Teal didn't know what to make of their conversation as she lay in her sleeping bag that night. He'd agreed with her, but then he hadn't said any more. After awhile she had changed the subject to lighten the mood between them. Nick had grown pensive and serious, and she felt badly about bringing him down. Obviously, he cared very much for his family. But there was something standing in the way.

Cooking the meal had lightened his mood, and by the time they had retired for the night they were back on an even keel. She snuggled down into the bag as far as she could and wriggled around to warm up all the corners. They hadn't had room to bring any propane heaters, so they were really roughing it. Luckily, the weather was warm for October, keeping them both pretty snug in their individual tents. The temperature dropped down to about fifteen degrees that night, but Teal didn't notice as she slept soundly after all the exercise she'd had that day.

They were up before the sun rose the next morning and hiked to their spot to wait for deer to pass by them. The ground was hard and it was all Teal could do to keep her teeth from chattering as they knelt on the cold soil. Her fingers and toes already felt like they were freezing from sitting so still.

She wished she could move just a little bit to keep her circulation going, but she knew that she had to stay motionless or she would scare the deer away.

After several hours, their diligence paid off, and Nick shot a beautiful buck. Teal hurried back for the horses while Nick cleaned and gutted the animal. It took quite awhile, but finally they got it back to their camp. It was too late in the day to ride out, so they decided to stay one more night. They kept the deer away from camp and hung it up from a tree to keep the surrounding wildlife from devouring it.

The temperature began to drop off before dark, and a gusty wind came up, making cooking over a fire almost impossible. "Looks like something's blowing in," Nick commented before they retreated to their tents.

"There wasn't anything in the forecast when we left."

"Even so, I'll bet money that there's snow on the ground in the morning."

Teal shivered at the thought. She was already freezing. "I hope not. That'll make it that much harder to get down in the morning."

Nick shrugged. "You can count on it being difficult either way. That wind isn't going to quit.

Packing our stuff up isn't going to be an easy chore.''

Teal was grateful to crawl inside her tent and get out of most of the wind. It was whipping the sides of her tent back and forth with a loud swooshing sound, and she wondered if she wouldn't be rolling down the mountain in it sometime that night. She climbed into her sleeping bag and watched her tent pitch back and forth. They'd tied the lines very securely, so she wasn't really worried about rolling, but the popping of her tent was so loud that she doubted she'd get any sleep.

She had to burrow down deep and pull her bag over her head to stay warm as she lived through what seemed like the longest night of her life. The howling wind tore at her tent all night, and she only managed to doze on and off. When she peeked outside at first light she found that Nick was right. A good inch of snow had already fallen, and by the way it was coming down it looked like they were in for a major winter storm.

Chapter Six

Nick had already rounded up the horses and was getting ready to saddle them. She ducked back inside and got dressed as fast as she could, and rolled up her sleeping bag. They skipped breakfast and just did the best they could to get everything packed up. It took them over an hour before they were finally ready to go. The snow was still coming down in large wet flakes, and visibility was down to about twenty feet.

"Are you sure we should try for it?" she yelled into Nick's ear, trying to be heard over the rush of the wind.

"We at least need to find a more protected place, if we don't make it all the way down. If visibility gets any worse we'll stop at the rock overhang that we passed on the way up."

She nodded her agreement and followed after him as he led his horse back down. They had

93

packed their belongings haphazardly in the wind, and now with the deer there was no room to ride.

The going got tougher as they slowly made their way down the mountain. The snow was accumulating rapidly, making visibility next to impossible. The wind was whipping the snow around in giant swirls, and it was beginning to drift in spots. Nick guided them around and through it until Teal lost all sense of direction and time. She knew that they were headed down, but she had no idea where they were or how much farther they had to go. The wind chill had dropped below zero, and the air was cutting into her like a knife. The horses were skittish and frequently balked, making the going that much slower.

Teal was just as afraid as the horses, but she did her best to keep her panic down. She had never seen a winter storm like this in October. It hadn't even been forecast. It was turning into a blizzard that would probably dump a foot of snow or more on them before it was over. If they didn't find shelter soon, she knew they wouldn't make it through the night. She tried not to think about it, concentrating only on keeping Nick's horse right in front of her.

Nick finally stopped and she drew up beside him. He turned to her and yelled into her ear. "We made it to the rock overhang. Take everything off your horse and let him go free—just in case.''

Teal nodded to let him know that she had heard him and understood. They wouldn't hobble the horses; letting them go free would give them the best chance to survive the storm. It was all she could do to get her pack off her horse. Her fingers were stiff and unbending, making it next to impossible to untie the leather straps on her saddle. Finally she was able to pull them free, and she lugged her pack off her horse and over next to the rocks where the wind wasn't quite so bad. She unsnapped the lead rope from her horse's halter and watched as he turned his tail toward the wind and moved in next to the rocks, taking advantage of the shelter they provided. Nick's horse huddled with him, and she prayed fervently that they would make it through the storm.

Nick was fighting to get his tent out, and Teal hurried over to help him. ''We'll just set up one,'' he yelled into her ear.

It was all they could do to get it up with the wind nearly pulling it out of their grasp and their fingers so stiff that they had trouble securing the lines. Eventually they conquered it and had it up well enough to hold against the onslaught of the storm. They pulled in both of their sleeping bags as well as their food supply, leaving everything else outside. The rocks were sheltering them from the worst of the wind, but their little tent couldn't protect them from the icy temperatures.

The sides of the tent would flap occasionally from a gust of wind, but for the most part they could hear one another over the noise. "Let's zip our sleeping bags together for added warmth," Nick suggested.

"That's a good idea, except that these bags won't zip together. The zippers are different sizes," Teal answered grimly.

Nick shook his head in frustration. "All right. Well, we'll both have to get into mine and we'll throw yours over the top. Our combined body heat ought to be enough to keep us warm until this blows over."

"Okay," Teal agreed.

They stripped off their heavy outerwear and hurriedly climbed into one of the sleeping bags. Nick unzipped the other bag and drew it over the top. It was a tight fit in one bag, but after a few minutes of shivering it began to warm up. Nick turned on his side and pulled her back into his stomach, fitting them together spoon fashion. He held her tightly to him until they both quit shaking.

"We're going to be all right," Nick assured her.

"I'm scared," Teal admitted. Her body continued to shiver sporadically, but now it was more from fright than from cold.

Nick rubbed her hands between his own and threw one of his legs over hers to let his body heat seep into her. "We'll stay warm enough in here to make it through. I know it's not comfortable, but it's the best we can do. There's nothing to be afraid of. We're going to make it just fine."

"I've never been caught in a blizzard before."

"Me either. So much for your mountain magic," Nick said, trying to lighten the tension. "If this is the kind of danger you were talking about, you can have it."

Teal could feel him laughing behind her as his stomach shook against her back. "I wasn't talking about this kind of danger. I could live without this myself." She was still a little bit too afraid to laugh with him or see the humor in it.

"I'm sorry I got you into this mess," Nick said seriously. "I'll do everything I can to get you out of it."

"It's not your fault. It was supposed to be warm for a week or more. I'm glad that you're not up here alone, actually. I'd be worried sick about you, if I were at home."

"Would you?"

His tone dropped with those words, and his voice became husky. She drew a breath sharply and realized that she couldn't deny it anymore. No man had ever affected her the way Nick did. He had kept her awake more nights than she could count, and just being with him every day meant the world to her. She had fallen in love with him and there wasn't anything she could do about it.

"Yes. I'd much rather be here with you than worrying about you out in this storm. I'd never forgive myself if something happened to you."

"Forgive yourself for what?"

Slowly she turned around in his arms until she was lying face to face with him. She drew her hand up and lightly ran her fingers down his cheek. "For not telling you how much you mean to me. I couldn't forgive myself if something happened to you before I could tell you how much I care about you. I've never met a man like you, Nick Marcus."

His eyes darkened as he reached up and ran his fingers lightly through her hair. "I've never met a woman like you either, Teal Berringer."

They moved as one until their lips were lightly brushing together. The cold was forgotten as they found a new warmth in one another. They melted together and lost all track of time as they explored this new and wondrous thing between them. Teal had never felt so much emotion, and their passion carried them together on a tidal wave of feeling.

They were both panting as they drew apart and

looked at each other. Nick smiled down into her face, and she couldn't remember when she had felt this happy. The fear of the storm was completely forgotten as she basked in the warmth of such wonderful feeling.

Nick was still very aware of the threat of the storm and had no intention of letting things get out of hand between them. This wasn't the time to get carried away by emotion. He had gotten them into this mess, and he was going to get them out of it—alive. "What made you change your mind?" he asked as he tried to rein in his galloping emotions.

Teal lazily circled a lock of his hair around her finger and smiled into his eyes. "I don't think anything made me change my mind. I've cared about you since the moment you came into my life, blasting Joe into the dirt for me. I've been afraid of losing you. You've made it clear that you only stay in one place for a year or so before moving on to the next ranch. If you're only going to stay for a year, I'd rather keep things on a business level. Or anyway, that's the way I was thinking."

"And now?" he prompted.

"And now I've realized that I have to live for the moment. I might not even be alive in a year. There aren't any guarantees in life, so I might as well enjoy every minute I have to the fullest and quit putting things off for a future of happiness.''

Nick knew that she had changed her mind because they were stuck in this blizzard. She was still assuming that they might not make it. ''We're going to survive this storm, Teal,'' he assured her. ''I'm glad that it changed your way of thinking, but we're going to live through it. I guarantee it.''

She snuggled in closer to him and lay her head on his shoulder as he rolled onto his back. She had to admit that she was cozily warm for the first time in what felt like days. They could still see their breath, but their sleeping bags were providing a warm little cocoon for them to rest in. ''At least I feel warm again,'' she admitted drowsily. ''If we can stay warm, we will make it. We've got plenty of food.'' She yawned loudly and snuggled closer. ''Are you hungry?''

Nick sighed and held her tighter. It felt so good to finally hold her in his arms like this that he felt like he didn't ever need to eat again. He had everything he wanted right here. ''Not right now. Let's try to get some sleep; we'll probably need to save all the energy we can.''

Teal closed her eyes and gave herself up to sleep, feeling completely protected in the shelter of his arms. She woke up later that afternoon as a draft of cold air hit her. She sat up with a start and looked around trying to figure out where she was. It all came flooding back as she saw Nick retying the tent flaps. He turned and hurried back in under the covers.

She could still hear the wind howling, and she shivered in reflex. "Has it stopped snowing?" she asked hopefully.

"Nope. It doesn't look like it's snowing as hard as it was this morning, but it's still coming down. It's really drifting up with this wind. It looks like we'll be spending the night here."

"What time is it?"

"It's about four o'clock in the afternoon. Why, did you have somewhere you needed to be?"

"Well yes, actually. I had a tea party to attend this afternoon," she answered in her best British accent. "My dear friend, Lady Margaret, is going to be so disappointed when I don't appear."

"I know how you hate to miss your tea parties. Do you suppose Lady Margaret will forgive you, if you tell her you were with me?"

"Don't be ridiculous. She thinks men are quite a bore. I'll have to tell her I was at some charity function or other." She sighed theatrically. "And not even a telephone to give her my apologies."

"We could always have a tea party of our own," Nick suggested. His stomach was growling, and he realized that he hadn't eaten since last night. "Are you hungry?"

"Famished," she said seriously as she dropped the accent.

"I'll get us something. You keep the bag warm." Nick crawled out again and dug through the bag of food, looking for something they didn't have to cook. He began to shiver immediately from the cold and hurried back with crackers, cookies, and some fruit.

It was difficult to eat and stay warm at the same time. They had to lie down to keep in the heat and the tight fit had them right on top of each other in the sleeping bag. Nonetheless, they made short work of the food and then settled in for the long night.

"I hope Millie isn't too worried about us," Teal said as she thought about what Millie must be going through.

"She knows we can take care of ourselves. She sure is one neat lady. My mouth is watering just thinking of the food she makes. I'm going to eat a ton when we get back," Nick said. The snack they'd just had felt like a mere hors d'oeuvre, and Nick's stomach was still waiting for the main course.

"I don't know what I'd do without her. She's

been like a mother to me ever since I can remember.''

''It's good that you had somebody to fill that role for you. Especially now that your father is gone.''

''I wasn't old enough to remember my mother very well, so it made it easier for me, I guess.''

''How old were you when she died?''

''I was only five. I have some vague recollections, but nothing real concrete. Of course, I have pictures of her, and I used to fantasize about her all the time. But with Millie there for me, I never felt deprived. I'm glad that I had my father as long as I did.''

Nick was impressed. Instead of feeling sorry for herself she had gotten on with her life. A lot of people would have used her situation to sit around and wait for handouts—like somebody owed her something because she'd had it rough. Not Teal, though. She sat here and said she was glad to have her father for as long as she did, rather than bemoaning the fact that he had been taken from her so early in life. It made him realize that he could have dealt with his own life better. Maybe his father had been right when Nick had left five years ago.

Teal was still curious about his family. She could tell from his expression that he was thinking about them again. She wished she knew more so that she could help him with it. "You said that your mother died. How old were you?" she asked. Maybe that would give her some clue about his problems.

Nick made an effort to snap out of his memories. "I was nineteen. I didn't go to college that year because she was really sick, and I wanted to spend as much time with her as I could. After she died, it was easier to stay home and help my father with the ranch. Until I felt that I needed to leave."

"So you stayed for two or three years before you started to wander around the country?"

"Three years."

"What made you change your mind?"

Nick sighed. She had a right to know, but he still didn't feel up to talking about it. He had held it in for five years, and he just wasn't ready to let go of it yet. The pain was eating him alive, but he'd work it out on his own. He was finally looking at it from his father's point of view, and from watching Teal he could see that he could have handled it better. Someday soon he would deal with it, but not right now. "My father and I had a difference of opinion, and I felt that it would be best for everyone if I left."

"Don't you think it's time you went back?"

"Soon. I will go back—soon. Just . . . not right now."

"You said your mother was sick. Couldn't the doctors do anything?"

"They did all they could. She had leukemia. Actually, she lived longer than they thought she would." Nick shuddered, remembering how difficult that time had been.

Teal hugged him close for comfort. She knew all about watching someone die. Watching her father fight that losing battle had torn her apart. At least she'd had the benefit of being older—being twenty-five had to be easier than dealing with it at nineteen. "I'm sorry."

"Yeah, me too. I like to think of her as being in a better place. Somewhere where she doesn't have to be weak or tired and can do whatever she wants to. Who knows—maybe from watching out for me she met your father. I think they would like each other."

"That's a nice thought. I'd hate for my father to be alone."

"You would?"

Teal sat up and looked into his eyes. "Why do you sound so surprised?"

"I figured you'd picture your father with your mother—not with mine."

"Oh, I see what you mean. Except that I never

really knew her and she's been gone for twenty years. It sounded better with your mom. Like they saw us together and approved or something like that. Other than Millie, I don't have any family for your family to meet.''

Again Teal had surprised him and made him look at his life differently. He had never wanted to see his father with someone else. Teal just wanted her father to be happy. Maybe that was the way it was supposed to be. If it were, he'd made a big mistake. He tried not to think about it as he answered, ''I've got enough family for the both of us. Believe me, once you meet them you'll understand. There may not be that many of them, but they sure have a way of filling up a house with their presence.''

''I'd like to meet them,'' she said simply.

''You will. . . . You will.''

Late that night the wind finally quit blowing, and Nick allowed himself to relax. He had been holding Teal close and watching her sleep for hours, just thinking about his life and wondering how he could put it back together. Once the wind stopped he knew that the storm had blown itself out. The temperature had dropped even lower, but at least the snow had stopped. They would be able to make it out in the morning. He sighed with relief and settled himself into a more comfortable position as he dropped off to sleep.

Early the next morning Teal woke to find herself snuggled against Nick's chest. She couldn't remember ever feeling this safe or this comfortable. Even though she was lying on the hard ground in just a sleeping bag it felt like pure heaven. She smiled to herself as she remembered him saying that she would meet his family. He hadn't told her that he loved her, but surely that was the next best thing. You didn't meet someone's family unless you were serious about them. Of course, she hadn't told him that she loved him either, but there was plenty of time for that. For now she was going to enjoy each day and let the future worry about itself.

She raised her head carefully and took a peek at Nick's face. He was sleeping soundly without a care in the world. His hair was curling all around his head in complete abandon, making him look macho with the three-day growth of beard on his face. His lashes looked even longer as they lay against the top of his cheekbones. He looked good enough to eat, and she giggled at the thought.

His eyes opened slowly and he growled at her, "What are you giggling about? And why are you staring at me?"

"Do you always wake up in such a good mood?" she pouted playfully.

"If I wasn't stuck in a cramped sleeping bag on the side of a mountain in a blizzard, I'd show you how much I appreciate being woken up by a beautiful woman. But under the circumstances you'll just have to forgive me."

She'd been awake for a good ten minutes, and she hadn't once thought of the storm. "Shhh . . . Listen."

Nick looked around, but he couldn't hear a thing. "What? I don't hear anything."

"That's just it. The wind has stopped. I bet we can get out of here."

"I know."

"What do you mean, you know? You just woke up."

"I was still awake last night when it stopped. I guess we should see how much snow is out there."

Teal shivered at the thought. "I don't want to go out there. Do you know how cold it is out there?"

"It's not warm, but we're not getting anywhere lying in bed."

They pulled their clothes into the sleeping bag with them and tried to thaw them out. They'd stripped down to their long underwear the day before, and now their jeans and shirts were frozen stiff by the cold.

"This is romantic," Nick said with a laugh as

he fought his way into his clothes without getting out of the bag. "I always wanted to spend a night with you in my long johns, and then beat you to death trying to get dressed the next morning. My wildest fantasies could never compare to the real thing."

Teal laughed until he elbowed her in the stomach, making her breath rush out in a whoosh. "Ouch," she protested.

"I'm sorry," he apologized. "I promise I won't hit you again—besides I'm all dressed."

"Thank goodness," Teal sighed gratefully.

Nick stopped thrashing around and smiled down at her. "Good morning, gorgeous."

She smiled back at him, thinking that waking up had never been so pleasurable. "Good morning yourself, handsome."

He dropped his head and kissed her lingeringly. When he pulled away, she was breathless. "I could get used to this," she said with a grin as she stretched her arms high over her head.

He grinned back slyly. "I'll make a note of it." He swatted her on top of the head as he finally crawled out and left her enough room to get dressed herself.

Chapter Seven

The sun was blinding as she stepped outside and looked around for Nick. The ground was swept clean around the rocks, but as she looked around she could see the snow piled two or three feet deep in places. The wind had blown so hard that it was difficult to tell just how much snow had fallen. It didn't really matter, though, since it wasn't deep enough to keep them from getting down to the truck and trailer.

One of the horses snorted, and she turned to see Nick leading them in. Icicles matted their hair and hung from their sides, but they really didn't look that much worse for wear. "Where were they?" she asked Nick as he approached.

"Just around on the other side of these rocks. The wind must have been blocked better over there. If I'd had more time yesterday, I would have put our tent up over there. We would have been a lot warmer."

"We made it through. It doesn't really matter," Teal assured him.

"Well, that's true. Let's get off this mountain. I'm freezing."

"Tell me about it."

They made quick work of repacking the horses and once again set off for the truck. Nick took the shortest route down and occasionally they had to fight their way through thigh-high drifts of snow. It was hard work, but they plowed on relentlessly, thinking only of a warm heater and soft clothes.

Even though Teal was freezing and panting from the effort of pushing through the snow, she'd never been happier. She had to squint her eyes nearly shut to block out the bright sunshine, but even that didn't dim her state of bliss. All was right with the world as she thought about how good it felt to be so attuned to Nick. He was everything she had ever looked for in a man. He'd already asked her about a partnership on her ranch. Surely that meant that he would be willing to stay here to work. He wouldn't find a better ranch anywhere, and she knew that he was aware of that. Of course, she was thinking of a lot more than just a business partnership, but there was plenty of time to talk about that. He'd probably want to settle things with his family first. That was just fine with her. Actually, she was kind of looking forward to having an extended family. What a concept.

When they finally made it back to the truck they had a difficult time getting it started and digging it out from under the snow. The snow plows had cleared the roads, but it was getting out to the road that was going to be quite a chore. They unpacked everything and loaded it into the back, but they left the horses off until Nick could make it to the road. He got stuck several times before the truck finally spun and lurched its way out onto the pavement. He left it running as he helped Teal load the horses into the trailer. There wasn't another soul around for miles, leaving the highway completely clear. They didn't have to worry about anyone running into them, but the lack of signs of civilization brought home to them how lucky they were to be alive.

The truck was so cold that they pulled into the yard just as the heater began to warm up. "It figures that the heater would start to work the minute we have to get out," Teal complained.

"I bet Millie will make us some hot chocolate," Nick offered.

"Oh, that sounds heavenly." Just the thought of it was enough to motivate her to get out. Everything, including the deer, was frozen, making it easy to just leave it all in the truck until Millie went to Fort Collins again and could drop the deer off at a shelter. They unloaded the horses and turned and looked down the road to the barn. That half mile looked like fifty miles—there was no way they could drive down there until they'd cleared the lane.

"I'll walk them down there," Nick offered. "You get that hot chocolate ready."

Just then Millie came flying out of the house all wrapped up in coats and scarves and boots. All they could see were her eyes as she ran up to them and engulfed Teal in a huge hug. She didn't say anything—she just held onto her as if for dear life.

Teal was touched by how much Millie must have been worried to show such a display of affection. She patted her back and assured her that she was all right. "I'm fine, Millie. A little cold maybe, but fine. I'm sorry that we worried you so."

Millie finally drew back and looked her over from head to toe. "My land, child. I've never been so frightened in my life. I've just been thinking about you two up there without any heat. How did you make it? I was ready to call out the police to start looking for you."

"I'll tell you all about it, but first we need to put the horses up in the barn. They need some grain and some warmth to help them recuperate.

It wasn't any more fun for them than it was for us.''

"Sakes alive! I've got coffee and hot chocolate on the stove and some chicken soup if you're hungry. You two go on in and get warm; I'll take care of these animals. I'm sweating from all these clothes as it is. You two go warm up now. Shoo!'' She waved her arms at them as she grabbed the lead ropes and began walking the horses down the lane.

Nick and Teal stared at each other for one astounded second before reality invaded and they made a run for the house. They stripped off their outerwear as fast as their numb fingers allowed and then made a beeline for the kitchen. They huddled together next to the stove and shivered as they leaned against one another. The soup and hot chocolate smelled delicious, but they were too cold to move another muscle.

Feeling finally returned and Teal's stomach began to protest with a vengeance. "I'll dish it up, you sit down,'' she commanded.

Nick wasn't in any mood to argue, but he moved away from the warmth of the stove with reluctance. They are slowly and savored every warm delicious bite as they warmed up from the inside out. Millie returned and bustled around, pampering them unashamedly. After awhile they all sat back with relief. "We made it," Teal said with a sigh.

"I told you we would," Nick said. Now that they were back, his natural confidence seeped back into his voice.

"I expect you to tell me all about it, but first a hot bath for the two of you. Nick, you can use the bathroom down here. I brought some of your clothes with me when I walked back from the barn. You two are going to stay inside and rest up for the rest of the day. Tomorrow will be plenty soon for you to be walking down to the trailer." Millie was in her element as she fussed over the two of them, making sure that they warmed up properly and were attended to.

Teal didn't have to be told twice. Just thinking about a warm bath made her skin tingle. Millie ushered Nick out to the downstairs bathroom while Teal hurried upstairs to her own. She didn't run the water very hot to start with since her skin temperature was still lower than normal. Even warm water felt hot to her touch, but once she lowered herself all the way in, her body began to acclimate. She added some more hot water and leaned back to relax. She was too tired to do anything but soak. Occasionally she leaned forward to add more hot water as she relaxed completely for the first time in three days.

After an hour, Millie knocked on her door. "Are you all right in there, Teal?"

Teal had been dozing lightly, and Millie's voice startled her. "I'm fine, Millie. Why? How long have I been in here?"

"About an hour now. Can I get you anything?"

"An hour?" Teal echoed in surprise. She looked at her fingers and noticed that her fingertips had begun to shrivel up like prunes. "No. I'm getting out now. I didn't realize I'd been in here that long. I must have dozed off or something."

"I'll have some hot tea waiting for you in the living room then. Do you want anything else to eat?"

The soup hadn't made much of a dent and her stomach was growling again. "Something light would be wonderful. We didn't eat much up there."

"All right. I'll fix something for you."

Teal washed off and toweled dry before slipping into a pair of black sweatpants with a matching sweatshirt. She pulled on a pair of warm woolly socks before slipping on a pair of slippers. She brushed out her hair and left it down before descending to the living room.

Nick was there ahead of her, propped up on some pillows with an afghan over his lower legs. "Don't you look comfortable," she commented just as Millie came in with a tray of snacks and some hot tea.

"Here you go," Millie said as she set everything down on the coffee table. "What else can I get for you?"

"Millie, you're a doll." Teal hugged her tightly. She drew back and said sternly. "Everything looks and smells wonderful, but you don't have to knock yourself out anymore. We'll be fine. If we need something, we'll get it ourselves. Why don't you sit down and relax with us?"

"Oh, I still have some things to put together for dinner. You two are the ones who need to relax. Sit down there with Nick and quit being bossy." As soon as Teal complied she bustled out of the room.

Teal looked at Nick. "I don't think I was being the bossy one, do you?"

"She's working off her stress. Let her get it out of her system. Besides, these snacks are wonderful. I'm finally starting to feel normal again."

"I always heard that the best way to a man's heart was through his stomach. I guess it must be true."

Nick laughed and grabbed her, pulling her close to his side. "Millie may have my stomach, but my heart is reserved for you."

Teal snuggled in close, feeling a warmth spread

through her. "You always did have a way with words."

"I've got a lot more where that came from."

"Well, don't use them all up at once." She smiled up at him playfully, hoping that he would quit talking and kiss her instead.

"Was that a hint?"

Teal sighed, realizing that she was going to have to take matters into her own hands. She reached up and held his face between her hands so that he couldn't get away. "Obviously it was too subtle for you." Before he could reply, she lightly touched her lips to his.

Nick didn't need anymore encouragement. He deepened the kiss and pulled her in closer, molding her body to his. All the days of denying how they felt about one another combined with the threat of the storm to release their emotions in one burst of passion. They were in danger of being consumed by it when Millie cleared her throat at the door.

Millie could see that more drastic measures were called for, and she cleared her throat one more time as loudly as she could. This time it made an impression on Nick and he raised his head. "Did you just hear a moose call?"

Teal was so dazed that she hadn't heard a thing and had no idea what he was talking about. "I think you're supposed to hear bells ringing, not a moose call. What does a moose call sound like?''

Millie cleared her throat one more time. These two were a lost cause.

''A moose call if I ever heard one,'' Nick said in triumph.

It was all Teal could do not to laugh. ''I think ringing bells would have been much more effective.''

''I'll keep that in mind,'' Millie said from the doorway. A moose call indeed.

Nick's chest began to shake and that was the last straw for Teal. She broke out in great peals of laughter as she turned in Nick's arms to look at Millie. The stern look on Millie's face didn't help, and Teal collapsed back against Nick as they both convulsed with glee. Millie did her best to keep the stern look intact, but she couldn't quite do it. One side of her mouth began to twitch, doubling Nick and Teal up even harder. Finally, Millie succumbed to the relief of it all and joined them in their hysterics.

Millie was the first to recover. ''A moose call,'' she said with disgust.

Nick tried to control himself. ''I'm sorry, Millie. I think that mountain magic has gone to my head or something.''

''I told you it would get you,'' Teal said, trying to be serious and failing miserably.

Millie could see that it was time to take charge. ''Dinner will be ready in about an hour. Do you need anything else before then?''

''I think we have everything we need,'' Nick answered. ''Thanks, though.''

''Hmmph,'' Millie said before she departed. It didn't surprise her in the least to see the two of them kissing on the couch. She was more surprised that it had taken this long. However, she could see that she had interrupted them at just the right moment. Anyway, Nick had certainly gotten the message. She knew that she owed it to Paul to keep an eye on his daughter. Teal probably wouldn't thank her for her interference right now, but she would some day.

''Millie has impeccable timing,'' Nick said.

Teal sighed with regret. ''Yes, I suppose that's one way of looking at it.'' She felt so good now that even an interruption wasn't going to bother her. ''So, what's on the TV?''

Nick flipped through the channels with the remote control while Teal settled herself more comfortably against his side. It felt so right to be lying there next to him. His arm fit snuggly across her shoulders and her hair tingled as his fingers gently played with it.

worried about being rejected. Her heart went out to him when she felt him shudder. ''You'll never know until you try.'' She wished she could encourage him better, but she just didn't know what had gone wrong. It was so frustrating to be kept in the dark.

Nick squeezed her in a brief hug. ''I know,'' he said softly. When she looked up at him he kissed her lips lightly. ''Watching you has shown me a lot of things. It's time that I try—just don't expect too much.''

''No matter what happens, I'll be here for you. You're not alone.'' It was as close as she could get to telling him that she loved him. Right now wasn't the time. He had to resolve this first before he could really concentrate on their relationship. She was going to do everything she could to support him without pressuring him.

Nick kissed the top of her head and squeezed her closer. ''That means a lot to me. Thank you.''

''Okay, you two,'' Millie announced from the doorway, ''dinner's ready.''

''Great,'' Nick exclaimed, ''I'm starved.''

''After all you've eaten this afternoon,'' Teal said in mock astonishment.

''I could eat a horse,'' he teased her. He knew that she would remember saying that before.

"I hope chicken will be a good substitute," Millie called as she led the way to the kitchen.

"Chicken is always better than horse in my book," Nick said as he laughed.

"Try not to eat too fast," Teal admonished. "I'd hate to give you a citizen's arrest on such a wintry day. Hauling you to jail could be quite a trial."

Nick held up two fingers. "Scout's honor. I'll eat as slow as humanly possible."

"I don't know, Millie. Do you think we should trust him? I mean, how do we know he was ever a boy scout?"

"On a day like this I think I'll take his word for it," Millie answered.

"Good idea," Nick said as he sat down at the table.

They all ate slowly, savoring every bite. To Nick and Teal it felt like ages since they'd had a good home-cooked meal. Millie was so glad to see them sitting at the table again that it was hard for her to swallow past the lump in her throat.

Once they'd finished eating they sat in companionable silence, sipping coffee and feeling mellow. Teal yawned and rubbed her eyes. "That was so good that I ate too much. I'm falling asleep in my coffee." Her emotions had swung on such a pendulum over the last few days—from fear of the storm to happiness about Nick—that now she was exhausted.

"I'm sure you're both worn out from your ordeal. Why don't you both give up and go get some sleep. There's no point in fighting it off when you've been under that much stress." Millie was feeling pretty worn out, too. If she could get these two to turn in, she could get to bed early herself.

"That sounds like a good idea," Teal answered. "I'll see you two in the morning."

Nick got up and walked with her. "Thanks for dinner, Millie," he said just before they walked out the kitchen door.

"You're welcome. Goodnight."

They wrapped their arms around one another as they walked toward the stairs. When they reached the banister, Teal turned to face him and leaned into his chest. Nick smiled lazily as he rubbed her hair back out of her face. "Are you going to sleep all right by yourself?" he asked.

A light lit in Teal's tired eyes. "I did kind of get used to sleeping next to you in that sleeping bag. My bed probably won't be as comfortable as you are."

"We'll have to do something about that real soon," he said just before he dipped his head and kissed her lingeringly. He drew back with great reluctance and said, "Goodnight, gorgeous."

It would have been so easy to stay there in his arms, but she forced herself to walk up the stairs. She looked back when she reached the top to see him still standing there watching her. "Goodnight, handsome." He smiled and she took that image of him with her as she slid into bed.

Chapter Eight

Teal slept a deep and dreamless sleep and didn't wake up until eight o'clock the next morning. She took her time getting dressed and meandered on down to the kitchen. Nick was just hanging up the phone in the hallway as she came down the stairs. He buried his face in his hands and Teal stopped in fear.

"Are you okay, Nick?"

He stiffened immediately and turned around. "I didn't know you were standing there," he said in a hoarse voice. All the color had left his cheeks, and he had a stricken look in his eyes.

She reached out and touched his arm lightly. "I just came down as you hung up. Was that your father you were talking to?"

Nick took a deep breath, visibly struggling to maintain control of his emotions. "No. That was my brother, Dave."

"Did he refuse to let you talk to your father? What's wrong, Nick?"

He shook his head and wiped his eyes, looking away from her. "My father wasn't there. I guess he's been in an accident."

His voice broke and he quit talking as he clenched his teeth together. Teal was really frightened now. "What kind of accident? When did this happen?"

"Dave said it happened yesterday. A drunk driver ran into his pickup. He's in the hospital now, and Dave isn't sure if he's going to make it or not."

Teal slid her arms around his neck and held him close. At first Nick held himself away from her, but after a moment he gave in to it and held her tightly. "He'll be okay," Teal whispered. "You have to hope for the best. I'll call and get us some plane tickets, and we'll be out of here this morning."

Nick was too grief-stricken to be capable of handling the details, making it easy to turn it all over to her. Teal led him into the kitchen and sat him down in a chair. "Millie, could you get Nick some strong coffee? His father's been in a car accident. I'm going to call and get us the first flight out to Oklahoma."

"My word," Millie exclaimed. "Of course."

She poured him a strong cup while they both watched him drink. He burned his tongue as it went down, snapping out of the haze he'd been in.

"Just get one ticket, Teal," he said hoarsely.

"I don't understand. Why one?"

"With this snow you're going to have to spread out some hay for the cattle. There's no way you can leave the ranch right now. That needs to be done first thing today. I'll be all right by myself. Don't worry. I was just shocked is all. My father has such a strong personality that it's difficult to picture him being injured."

Teal wanted to argue, but she knew what he said was true. There was no way she could leave the ranch unattended right now. "Okay, I'll go call the airlines. You drink the rest of that coffee."

The first flight out that he could make from Denver was at four o'clock that afternoon. Teal booked him on it and hurried back into the kitchen with the news. "Your plane leaves at four. That gives you plenty of time to pack some clothes and drive down to Denver. I'll give you a ride down to the trailer and help you pack."

They unhooked the horse trailer and Nick drove the pickup down the lane. The snow was packed hard from the wind, but the pickup sat up high enough that they didn't have any problem making it down. Nick warmed up his own four-wheel-drive pickup while Teal went inside to organize his clothes. It was a four hour drive, and he needed to be there an hour before his flight, which didn't leave them much time.

When they had everything he needed packed up they paused to look at one another in the doorway. "Call me when you get there," Teal said softly, "just to let me know how everything is."

Nick nodded. "I will."

"You better get going."

Nick nodded again. Tears welled in Teal's eyes, and Nick dropped his duffel bag to gather her close. He kissed her roughly, letting out his emotion in the only way he knew how. Teal responded just as roughly as the tears escaped her eyes and slowly ran down her cheeks.

After a while Nick forced himself to draw back. He wiped her tears from her face with his fingers and smiled sadly. "I'll be all right. Don't worry about me. Believe me when I tell you that I'll be back."

Teal nodded, unable to speak. She knew that he wanted to come back now. But if his father were to die, there could be all kinds of reasons for him to stay in Oklahoma. She had no idea what the problem with his family was, and she had no way to know if he would come back or not.

He pulled her back in tightly and then kissed her one more time. "Goodbye, gorgeous."

She sucked her breath in on a sob as she forced out, "Goodbye, handsome."

He turned and ran for his truck, wanting to hide his own tears from her. She watched from the doorway as he drove up around the hill and was gone. She slid down the wall and huddled on the floor as she let out all her fear and pain. She cried for Nick and for his father and could only hope that everything would turn out all right.

After a long while she regained her composure and realized that she had work to do. She'd watched her father pick up the round rolls of hay to feed to the cows—surely it wasn't that difficult. It took her most of the day to figure it out, but by nightfall she had spread out plenty of hay for the herd for one night. Now that she knew what to do, it wouldn't be too much trouble to drive around and feed the cattle each day.

She hurried in just before dark, wanting to be in the house in case Nick called. "Have you heard anything, Millie?" she asked as she stripped off her insulated coveralls.

"No. The phone hasn't rung all day. Dinner's almost ready. Come on into the kitchen and have some coffee with me."

The day had been frosty and cold, making the

thought of something warm to drink most appealing. Her cheeks were a bright red from the cold air and the wind, but even the color in her face didn't make up for the dullness in her eyes. She sat down heavily with a sigh. "I hope his father's all right."

"I'm sure Nick will let us know the minute he knows anything. He's a strong man, he'll be just fine," Millie assured her.

"He hasn't seen his family in five years. Something went wrong back then that he won't tell me about. He was calling this morning to see how they were doing. If something happens to his father, I'm not sure that he'll survive the guilt of being gone for so long."

Millie sighed. "Don't go borrowing trouble where there isn't any. Did Nick tell you what happened?"

"Just that his father was hit by a drunk driver yesterday. He's in the hospital and his brother Dave wasn't sure if he was going to make it or not."

"It's a good thing that he called when he did. How come they didn't call here for him?" Millie asked.

"He hasn't told them where he is. He only sends a Christmas card once a year."

"My land, how awful." Millie shuddered. "No

one should get so estranged from their family. What an awful thing to have happen.''

''He said he'd call when he got there. I guess in the meantime we just wait.''

The day passed in a haze as Nick drove down the Poudre Canyon and then down I-25 to Denver. He called his brother from the airport to let him know his flight number and managed somehow to survive the wait until he got there.

He slung his bag over his shoulder as he walked off the plane. Both of his brothers were waiting for him as he entered the airport. They engulfed him in a huge bear hug, and he held onto them for dear life.

Dave was the first to recover. ''It's good to see you, Nick.''

Nick took a deep breath before he answered. He had expected them to be angry with him for being gone. Dave's simple statement had him close to tears again. ''It's good to see you too, Dave. You still look the same as the last time I saw you.'' Dave was six feet tall, 180 pounds, with darker brown hair than Nick and blue eyes. His hair was cut short, but the ends still curled out under his battered black cowboy hat.

Andrew squeezed his shoulder and said gruffly, ''We've missed you, bro.'' His light brown hair was covered by a tan cowboy hat that shaded his brown eyes and long eyelashes. He was an inch shorter than Nick, but of the three he was the most handsome. He had a baby face that belied his true age, and such a mild manner that women fell all over him no matter what he did.

Nick threw his arms around him and hugged him tightly, not caring that they were standing in the aisle and that people were pushing their way past them. ''I missed you too, my man. You're looking good.''

Dave grabbed his duffel bag and said, ''Come on. Let's get out of here.''

They walked through the airport three abreast, Nick in the middle. Together they presented an image of husky, tough guys, and people made an effort to get out of their way. ''How's Dad?'' Nick asked fearfully.

''He's still hanging in there,'' Dave answered.

''He's been asking for you,'' Andrew said quietly.

Nick was shocked. He hadn't expected his father to think about him at all—not after the way they had parted five years ago.

''What made you call?'' Dave asked. ''I mean, after all this time—why today?''

''Not because I knew that something was wrong. I met somebody who got me to thinking about it all from another point of view. I guess I wanted to see if Dad would talk to me after all this time.''

"He's been regretting it ever since you left. If you had let him know where you were he would have come to see you. But you never sent a return address or told any of us where you were. Once a year he found out you were still alive, but he couldn't ever reach you.'' Dave's voice was matter of fact. He was just reciting the way it was, not blaming or judging him.

"I wasn't ready for that until today,'' Nick answered. "I hope it's not too late.''

"It's never too late,'' Andrew said. "We'll take you straight to the hospital and you can talk to him then.''

"Is he conscious?''

"Some of the time,'' Andrew answered.

When they got to the hospital Dave and Andrew led the way to his room. Nick stopped ten feet from the door when he saw Misty huddled on a bench, staring at the floor. Her blond hair was hiding her face, and her small body looked forlorn as she waited there by herself.

Dave kept walking and asked her how their father was doing. "His condition hasn't changed,'' she answered as she looked up. "The doctors are beginning to think that's a good sign.''

Nick realized that here was one who had

changed in the last five years. She looked older and more mature as she talked to Dave. Her voice was deeper and she seemed to have gained a poise that had been lacking when he'd known her before. She was a year younger than he was, but she had always seemed like such a kid to him. Now she looked like a woman, and he was struck by the change in her.

Andrew had stayed beside Nick and now he pushed him forward. "Come on," he encouraged.

Nick walked forward. "Hello, Misty."

She just stared at him in shock. He was the last person she had ever expected to see here. "How did you find him?" she asked Dave.

"We didn't. He called us."

She turned back to Nick and waited, expecting him to yell or do something violent. When he didn't she looked at him in puzzlement. "What are you doing here?" Her voice only held curiosity. None of the animosity of years before was there.

Nick couldn't believe the change in her. Before, she had been spoiled and her face had been twisted in hatred every time she looked at him. Now there was a serenity about her, and her hair fell about her pretty face in soft abandon. She wasn't anything like he remembered her. He began to wonder if he hadn't just imagined a lot of that anger out of his own sense of hurt and betrayal.

His father had married this girl three years after his own mother had died. At the time, he had been outraged. She was a year younger than he was, and too immature and childish to be real. He couldn't believe his father would do something like that. He had baited her and argued with her constantly, believing that the only reason she was there was for security and for the money she would get when his father died.

His father had tried to explain it to him, but he had never listened. His father had defended Misty to him, and for that he thought he'd never be able to forgive him. He'd left, never to return—until now.

He cleared his voice and answered her. "I came to see my father."

"Every time he wakes up he asks for you," she said. "Go on in. Just try not to tire him. He's incredibly weak."

Nick looked toward the door. He took a moment to gather his courage before walking in. The monitors were making a soft humming noise as he closed the door behind him. He moved over to the bed and looked down at his father. His head was swathed in bandages, and his right arm and leg were encased in casts. An IV was attached to his other arm as well as various other kinds of wires that Nick had never seen before. Matt's face was bruised and blotched purple, distorting him so much that Nick never would have recognized him on his own.

An overwhelming sense of guilt and helplessness attacked him as he stood looking down at his father. So many years had been wasted to end like this. He sat down next to the bed and grasped his father's left hand. "I'm sorry, dad," he whispered painfully.

Matt squeezed his fingers and Nick looked up through his tears to find his father's eyes open and looking at him. "Nick," he whispered hoarsely.

"Yes, dad. It's me, Nick."

Matt coughed painfully and Nick reached for a glass of water and helped his father drink through a straw. After a few sips he lay back with relief. "How did they find you?" he asked in a raspy whisper.

"I called. I didn't know. But I got here as soon as I could. You're going to be just fine. Hang on, dad."

His father waved his hand in dismissal of all that. "I've looked for you for years. I did the wrong thing, yelling at you the way I did. If I could have found you, I would've apologized to you. I handled it all wrong. So sorry," he wheezed.

"No, dad. Save your energy. You don't need to explain anything. It was me. I was wrong to leave like that. It's not your fault."

"You were still grieving for your mother. We never talked about that, you and I."

"I was such a dumb kid," Nick said in a totally broken voice, tears running unashamedly down his face. He was too afraid that his father was going to die to care. "It was me, dad. I wouldn't listen to you. It didn't matter what you did. I was wrong, and I'm sorry."

Matthew released his son's hand to pat Nick's cheek. "I love you, son."

"I love you too, dad."

What little energy Matt seemed to have gave out and he lay back limply as his hand fell to the bed. Nick looked up in a panic, but the monitors still showed a steady heartbeat; his father had just fallen asleep. He stayed for a few minutes as he regained his composure and wiped his face. A nurse came in to check on Matt, and Nick got up to leave.

His brothers were waiting for him when he came out. "How's he doing?" they asked at the same time.

"He talked to me for awhile, but he's sleeping now."

"Did he get to say everything that he wanted to?" Misty asked.

"I don't know. I think so," Nick answered. He leaned heavily against the wall and closed his eyes in exhaustion.

"You must be awfully tired if you got here in one day," Misty observed. "Why don't we go get something to eat in the cafeteria. If he's sleeping now, it'll be awhile before he wakes up again."

"That's a good idea," Andrew agreed. He grabbed Nick around the neck with his arm and led him off down the hall.

Once they'd all gotten what they wanted to eat, they sat down at a corner table. "So who's the girl?" Dave asked.

Nick looked up from his plate. "Are you talking to me?"

"Yeah. Who's the one that made you call home today?"

"She didn't make me call. How did you know she was female? I didn't say anything either way."

"I just figured it was. So, who is she?" Dave wasn't going to let Nick sidetrack him. He hadn't seen his brother in five years—he wanted to know everything there was to know.

"Her name is Teal."

"And?"

Nick sighed. "And she lives in Colorado, and I was helping her run her 200-acre ranch there."

"What's she like?" Andrew asked.

"She's brave," Nick said after he thought for a moment. "Life has dealt her one rotten hand after the other, yet she still goes on with a positive attitude. Nothing gets her down for long. She thinks that ranching is the greatest thing on earth."

"Some girl," Dave said with surprise. She sounded perfect for Nick.

"Yeah, she is," he agreed.

"I suppose you were hoping that I'd be gone by now," Misty interrupted.

Nick looked at her for the first time since he'd sat down. "No. Actually, I was hoping just the opposite."

Misty's mouth dropped open in surprise, and Andrew coughed in reaction. "You were?" she asked, dumbfounded.

"Teal's father died this summer, and she told me that she liked to think of him with someone. She didn't want him to be alone, and she said she wanted him to be happy. It made me think that I had never thought that for my father. All I had thought about was myself. It wasn't you so much that I was angry with. Any woman would have caused the same reaction. It wasn't fair of me, and I apologize."

Misty couldn't speak and Dave filled the gap by shaking Nick's shoulder. "It takes a strong man to admit when he's been wrong. I'm proud of you, my man."

Nick nodded at him and smiled.

"You were the closest one to mom," Andrew said quietly. "But you never would talk about her. You always kept everything inside, which isn't like you at all. It had to come out sometime, somehow. Don't be too hard on yourself now. Dad wouldn't want that."

"No, he wouldn't," Misty said as she wiped her eyes with a shaky hand. "I handled it poorly myself, so I have to take most of the blame. I didn't know how to deal with you, and everything was so new to me that I broke down a lot and got defensive too easily. I've always wished that you would come back so that I could apologize to you. I'm sorry, Nick. I hope that you will look at this as your home again, and stay here if you want."

Nick nodded and looked down. After a moment he looked back to meet her gaze. "Thank you."

Dave and Andrew caught him up on everything that had happened since he'd left. The atmosphere at their table was a lot less tense as they finished eating. When he was through, Nick excused himself. "I need to make a telephone call. Is there a phone I can use for long distance here?"

Misty dug in her purse and handed him several dollars worth of quarters. "There's a pay phone right over there."

Nick thanked her and walked to the phone. Teal answered on the second ring. "Hello?"

"Hi, gorgeous."

"Nick," she breathed with relief. "How are you?"

"I'm fine now. I got a chance to talk to my father; he's still hanging in there, but I guess he's not out of the woods yet."

"Did you tell him everything you wanted to?" she asked with concern. She knew how important it would be for him to do that, especially if his father died.

"I did. I'll tell you all about it when I get back."

"You're going to stay until he's better though, aren't you?"

"Yeah. I need to stay for awhile. Are things okay there without me?"

"No problem. The cattle are all fed. Don't worry about me—you just take care of everything out there."

"Okay. Listen, I don't have any more quarters and the operator is going to break in soon. I'll call you again in a few days. Okay?"

"Take care of yourself, handsome," she said,

wishing she felt comfortable enough to tell him that she loved him.

"You too, babe. Goodbye."

"Bye."

Nick hung up the phone and stared at it for a few seconds. He had wanted to tell her that he loved her, but he wanted the first time to be in person. He had no idea how long he would be here. He knew that it wasn't fair to her, but what else could he do?

Chapter Nine

T eal found plenty of things to keep her busy as she waited each day for Nick to call. Their conversations were growing more stilted by the day, and it worried her. When they were together they could talk about anything, but this separation was taking its toll. They were both doing their best to avoid the issue of love or even of being together, leaving them almost nothing to talk about. Teal asked after his father and his family, but other than that she didn't know what to say. He still hadn't told her what was going on, and it was too awkward to ask him about it when they were talking long distance.

She found a lot of satisfaction in being able to handle the ranch by herself, but she missed the camaraderie she'd had with Nick and the way they had always made a game out of everything they did. Her fears were beginning to mount higher and higher as she imagined the worst—that he would never come back.

He'd only been gone for five days, but it felt like an eternity as she waited for his call that night. She felt so helpless waiting by the phone. It seemed like there must be something she could do, but she didn't know what.

She grabbed the phone the minute it rang and shakily said, "Hello." His calls were beginning to make her nervous, and she knew that was a bad sign.

"Hi, Teal. It's me."

"Hi, Nick. How are things going today?"

"About the same. Dad is still really weak. He's not in critical condition anymore, but he still has a long way to go. He's battling some kind of infection, and the doctors don't really know when he'll be completely out of the woods."

"Are you still able to talk to him?"

"Every now and then. We've been taking turns sitting with him. He sleeps most of the time."

"You just have to think positively. All you can do is hang in there."

"Yeah, I guess so."

He sounded so distant and detached that Teal's heart jumped in reaction. She was losing him and there wasn't a thing she could do about it. "Things are going well here," she offered in a tone slightly higher than her own. She cleared her throat and went on, "The weather has been clear since you left, making it pretty easy to get around now. Hopefully it'll stay dry for awhile."

"That's good. I'm glad you're doing all right by yourself." Actually he wasn't in the least bit glad. He liked it when she depended on him for things. He knew he was being unfair since he couldn't possibly be there now, but it would be nice to hear that she needed him back. His mind knew that she was just being upbeat for his sake, but his heart wanted to hear how much she missed him. He hated to think that this separation was easy for her.

He didn't sound like he was the least bit interested in what she was doing. He sounded like he was getting along with his family—maybe planning to stay there. Distancing himself from her would make it easier for him to tell her that he wasn't coming back. Her negative thoughts were eating her alive! "Yeah well, hang in there." She wanted to tell him to hurry back, but that would just make him feel guilty. She sighed heavily. "Let me know if there's any change or anything I can do."

"Sure. Listen, I better go now. Take care of yourself."

"I will. You too."

"Okay. Bye."

"Bye."

She laid the receiver down lightly and rested her head against the wall. They didn't even use their familiar greetings and goodbyes anymore. More than likely it was over. Somehow she was going to have to get used to that fact. She moaned softly thinking about it. This was worse than anything she'd dealt with before. She'd gotten over her fear of Joe, and she was handling her grief over her father, she was even running the ranch by herself, but this—this seemed insurmountable.

Millie walked out of the kitchen, looking for her. "Oh, there you are. Are you all right?" She laid her hand on the back of Teal's neck. "What is it?"

Teal turned away from the wall and hugged Millie quickly. "I'm okay," she said as she stepped back. "What's for dinner?"

Millie could see that she wasn't in the least bit okay. Her eyes were rimmed with dark circles, evidence that she hadn't been sleeping. And she knew very well that she wasn't interested in dinner, since she had hardly eaten anything since Nick had left. "Was that Nick you were talking to?"

"Yes. No change, he says. His father is fighting off an infection of some kind. Looks like he'll be in the hospital for quite some time yet." She did her best to make her voice sound normal, but it rang false even to her own ears.

Millie led her into the kitchen and made her sit down at the table. She took a seat beside her and ordered, ''All right. Out with it. What is really going on? You need to talk about it, and you know I'm a good listener. Besides, who else are you going to talk to?''

''Oh, Millie,'' Teal sighed as she dropped her forehead into her palm.

''Don't 'Oh, Millie' me. Come on—what gives?'' She knew that if she softened her voice and offered sympathy that Teal would just fall apart, so she used the hard tack instead.

''I don't think Nick is coming back.''

''Why not? Did he say that in so many words?''

''It's more what he hasn't said than what he has. He's distant and aloof. He used to greet me by calling me gorgeous. Now it's just, 'Hi, Teal.' ''

''He's got a lot on his mind. Things could be a lot rougher out there than he's telling you. Maybe he's just trying to spare you by not dumping his feelings on you. Is that possible?''

Teal thought about it for a moment. ''It's possible, I guess. It's just not like him to sound like that. I think he's trying to distance himself to make it easier to tell me he's not coming back.''

''Have you told him how much you're looking

forward to his coming back? Or even how much you miss him? How about love—do you tell him you love him?'' It was obvious from Teal's despondent look that Millie had to pull out all the stops. She was being rough on her, but it was the only way to snap her out of this passiveness she'd fallen into.

Teal sat back and looked at Millie in surprise. ''Well, no. But I don't want him to feel guilty or anything about this place or me. He's got so much to worry about that I thought I'd be supportive instead of dumping on him.''

''Isn't telling him you love him being supportive? You do love him, don't you?''

She was making a statement, not asking a question, and Teal knew it. She sighed again. ''Yes. I love him, and I suppose it would be supportive. Oh, what a mess. I didn't want to pressure him. What if he doesn't love me? He hasn't ever said that he does.''

''I'm sure he would have, if this hadn't come up to take him away.''

''You think so?''

Millie shook her head with disgust. ''Girl, that boy is so far gone over you it isn't funny. He's got love dripping out of every pore. So do you, but the two of you are too busy dancing around one another to realize it. I've never seen such tomfoolery. Tell the man you love him. What do you have to lose?''

She'd never thought of it like that. She really didn't have anything to lose. If he wasn't coming back, he wasn't coming back. Maybe he did need to hear it. It was worth a try.

''Why don't you go out there and tell him in person,'' Millie suggested.

What a great idea! she thought. No, wait a minute. ''I can't. I have to feed the cattle.''

''I've been watching you. It takes quite a while to feed one of those bales. Hoist one up on the truck for me and I'll feed every day until you get back. Of course, you can't be gone for more than a couple of days, but that should be plenty of time.'' Millie sat back with a satisfied grin. This giving advice wasn't so hard.

Teal sat in astounded silence for a second before she jumped up with a loud war whoop. ''Millie, you are the greatest!'' She picked Millie up out of her chair and swung her around the room in exuberance.

Millie hung on in fright. She outweighed Teal by twenty-five pounds. She wasn't so sure that Teal wouldn't collapse on the floor with her on top. ''Put me down,'' she gasped.

Teal complied and swatted her on the arm. ''How come I never thought of that?''

"You haven't been around as long as me, dearie." She patted her hair back into place and adjusted her clothes. "Warn me before you ever try that again," she admonished.

They smiled at one another. "I love you, Millie."

"I love you too, girl. Now get out of here. I've got dinner to fix."

Teal skipped out of the kitchen and began making plans to leave the next day.

Nick felt just as depressed as Teal when he hung up the phone. She had said that she wasn't ready for a relationship. Now that he was gone, was she beginning to regret how personal she'd become with him? He wished he knew.

"What's up?" Andrew asked as he walked into the den. Nick had been staying at his father's, and everyone naturally gravitated there to hear the day's news.

"Nothing going on here," Nick answered. "How's dad?"

"Still the same," Andrew answered as he switched on the TV. He had just left the hospital and Misty was taking a turn sitting with Matt. "Were you just talking on the phone?"

"Yeah."

"So, how are things in Colorado?"

"Seems to be going just fine without me," Nick answered in a despondent tone.

"You pretty serious about this girl?"

"What makes you ask that?"

"That hang-dog look you've got on your face since you hung up."

"Oh."

Andrew looked at him seriously. "So, what's stopping you?"

"How does 'She's there and I'm here' grab you for an answer?"

"As soon as dad gets better you can go back. Doesn't she know it isn't going to be forever?"

"I don't know. I was thinking of staying for awhile when dad comes home. Try to make up for lost time or something."

"Hey. Hold on there. Now that you've worked it out, you can come visit him all the time. Who said you had to give up your entire life to atone for the last few years?"

Nick drummed his fingers on the desk in agitation. "I just feel like I owe it to him."

"He's been feeling like he owes you something ever since you left. You both made some mistakes. Don't make it worse by trying to make up for it. Let it go."

Nick sighed. It sounded nice the way Andrew put it, but it wasn't that easy. "We're kind of getting ahead of ourselves here. Dad hasn't come home yet.''

''He's a tough old bird. He'll come home. Once Misty tells him her news, he'll recover like a shot.''

Nick sat up at that. ''What news?''

Andrew studied him for a moment. ''I'm sure she wanted to tell you herself, but I don't suppose you're going to let me get away with that.''

''You're right. I'm not.''

Andrew nodded. ''I thought you'd say that. She's going to have a baby.''

Nick's eyes widened as he sat there digesting that one. ''A baby, huh?''

''Another kid in the family. Maybe it'll be a girl. I always wanted to say that I had a sister.''

''You seem to be happy about it,'' Nick commented. He didn't know what to think himself.

''Sure. Why not? She says that they've been trying for months, so obviously it's okay with dad. If it makes him happy, why not?''

Why not indeed? Andrew seemed to look at life like Teal did, which amazed Nick, since he'd never realized it before. ''I guess you're right,'' was all he said in response.

Teal ran around the house like a chicken with its head cut off as she tried to get ready to leave the next day. She had to make reservations, pack, and take care of all kinds of odds and ends. First thing in the morning she would get a load of hay ready for Millie, and then she could leave. When she finally had it all taken care of, she was too wired to go to bed. She wandered into the living room and sat down next to Millie, who was watching the ten o'clock news.

"Anything besides drugs and murder on tonight?" Teal asked with sarcasm. She hated to watch the news these days; they always seemed to find the most violent stories possible to put on their shows.

Millie waved her hand to shush her. "They're talking about the weather."

The meteorologist on channel nine was just getting wound up about a big blizzard coming into the area that night. "The mountains can expect to get anywhere from six inches to a foot of snow tonight with more falling tomorrow," he said as his voice rose in excitement. He looked like this storm was the highlight of his career. "We don't expect quite that much down here in Denver and along the plains," he said as he pointed to his map. "We're expecting about four inches by morning and somewhere between eight and twelve inches by the time this storm leaves the area. It's a slow-moving band of low pressure, and you can expect to see it hang around Colorado for at least two days.''

Teal looked at the TV like it had gone crazy. He was talking about a major blizzard. This wasn't possible. Her plane was leaving at six o'clock the next evening. The way he made it sound she couldn't possibly get down the mountain. ''Do you mind if we watch channel seven?'' she asked Millie. ''Maybe they're saying something different.''

Millie nodded her head in agreement and Teal jumped up to change the channel. They were in the middle of the weather forecast and this weatherman was telling the same story. He had that same excited look on his face as the other one. It must make their day to finally have some weather to talk about, Teal thought in disgust. Channel four wasn't any different, and Teal shut the television off with a sharp snap. ''This is ridiculous. It can't possibly snow that much overnight. Have they been talking about this for long?'' She hadn't been watching the television at all in the last few days. All she had thought about was Nick.

''They mentioned it a couple of days ago when I watched last,'' Millie answered. ''But they hadn't known how much it was going to snow then. They said they were keeping their eye on it or something like that.''

Teal moved over to the windows and looked

out. The branches on the trees were swaying at a pretty good clip and she could hear the rush of the wind now that she was paying attention. How could this happen? "It's starting to blow already." If she left right then she could probably make it down to Denver, but she didn't have the hay ready yet. She couldn't expect Millie to take care of that on top of everything else. She still wasn't that good at it herself. She needed the light of day to see by or she wouldn't get it done. "I guess I can always hope that it doesn't snow that much," she said despondently.

"That's an awfully long drive to make even in good weather. If it is snowing, I don't think you should try it," Millie said with worry sounding in her tone. She still hadn't recovered from the last storm when she had worried so much about Teal.

Teal knew that she couldn't expect Millie to feed the cattle if it was snowing as hard as they predicted. Not to mention the fact that driving to Denver would be next to impossible. More than likely the airport would shut down anyway. The plains rarely saw much snowfall in late October, but there was always a first time. "When has Denver ever gotten a blizzard in October?" Teal asked hopelessly.

"If you had left the TV on they probably would have told us that," Millie commented. "Seems like they're always talking about the airport being jam packed with people at Thanksgiving because a storm has slowed down the flights or stopped it all together.''

''Well, that's in November,'' Teal argued.

''Not a whole lot of difference, since this is the end of October.''

''Maybe they're wrong. Whenever they predict a lot of snow, we never get any. We always get a lot when they say we're not going to get much.''

''That's true,'' Millie agreed.

But as it turned out, the weathermen were right. When Teal woke up the next morning there was six inches of new snow on the ground and more coming down at an incredible rate. She couldn't even see her pickup, parked out beside the house.

She walked slowly into the kitchen and poured herself a cup of coffee. ''I guess I won't be going anywhere,'' she said. She didn't sound quite as frustrated and depressed as she had the night before.

''I thought you'd be a little more upset,'' Millie commented.

One thing that Teal had gotten used to over the years was the unpredictability of the weather in Colorado. People that had lived in the state for years were fond of saying that if you didn't like the weather, wait a couple of hours and it'd be different. "It's not the end of the world. When I get all the chores done, I'll give Nick a call. It won't be the same as talking to him in person, but it'll have to do."

"That's the spirit." One of the things that Millie had always admired about Teal was her ability to bounce back from disappointments. Her adaptability was one of her strongest traits.

Teal could hardly see in front of her when she went outside. She drove off the path several times because she couldn't see where the road was with snow flying in a million different directions. She managed to get unstuck each time but it was late in the day by the time she had all the hay spread out for the cattle.

She was bone tired by the time she collapsed in front of the fireplace that afternoon. Millie had a cheerful fire going and was quick to bring her something to eat and drink. "I'm glad you made it in before dark. I was getting worried about you."

"I was lucky to get it done at all. There must be a foot of snow out there." She rubbed her eyes in exhaustion as she put her feet up close to the fire. "Did Nick call?"

"No, not yet. I bet he'd like to have you call him," Millie suggested.

Now that the time was upon her, Teal was nervous about talking to him. Her doubts were assailing her again, and she was more afraid than she was willing to admit. "Yeah, I guess you're right," she said without much enthusiasm.

"Just tell him how much you miss him and want him back. You'll be pleasantly surprised at his reaction. I guarantee it." Millie had plenty of confidence for both of them.

Teal gathered her courage and approached the phone like a soldier going into battle. Once she dialed the number he'd given her, she waited with her heart pounding at ninety miles an hour. A woman answered the phone and for a second Teal didn't know what to say.

"Anyone there?" the woman asked again.

"I'm sorry," Teal explained. "I'm looking for Nick Marcus, but I must have the wrong number."

"No, you have the right one. Hold on a minute and I'll get him."

Teal could hear her calling for him in the background and she wondered who the woman was. Nick had only talked about his father and his two brothers. Who was the woman? Maybe she was the housekeeper or something, although she hadn't answered the phone like an employee would.

She didn't have much time to think about it before Nick answered, "Hello?"

"Hi, Nick. This is Teal," she explained unnecessarily.

Nick was surprised to hear from her. This was the first time she'd ever called him. Immediately he thought the worst. "Is something wrong?"

"I just wanted to talk to you. Everything's fine here." She paused for a second, thinking of Millie's advice. It was worth a try. "Actually, it's really rotten here without you. We're having a blizzard here, and it took me all day to get hay to the cattle. All I could think was how cold and awful it was, but then I thought about you, and I knew that if you were here you would have made a game out of it or something, and it wouldn't have been a big deal at all. I wish you were here."

Nick took a second to let all that soak in—it felt so good to hear her say that she missed him that he wanted to savor it for awhile. His silence scared her until he answered, "I miss you, too." Before she could absorb that he went on, "You shouldn't go out in a blizzard by yourself. What if you had gotten lost?"

She was so relieved that she burst out laughing.

"What's so funny? I'm telling you that it's dangerous to go out in a blizzard and you laugh. I can't believe you."

He was finally talking to her with emotion in his voice. In fact, he sounded just like his old self. She didn't even care that he was treating her like a child. He cared and that's all that mattered. "I'm sorry. It's just good to hear you sounding like yourself again. Has your father gotten better?''

He forgot all about the weather as he got excited to tell her the good news. ''Dad was feeling well enough to sit up and drink some fluids today. He seems to have beaten the infection and now all he has to do is regain his strength.''

''That's great, Nick. I'm really glad to hear that; I've been so worried about you.''

Immediately Nick felt guilty for what he had to say next. ''Even though he's getting better, I don't feel like I can come back yet. I feel like I need to be here for him for awhile. I just can't get away right now.''

That made sense to Teal. They'd been apart for five years; of course he would feel the need to stay. Here was her chance to be supportive. ''I understand. I'm sure your father needs all of you around him now until he gets back on his feet. It isn't as much fun here without you, but I'm taking care of the basics. You take as much time as you need.''

''You wait until that storm is over before you go outside again,'' he admonished. ''And Teal—thanks.''

''It's supposed to subside tomorrow, so don't worry. I better let you get back to your family.''

''Yeah. I don't want to run up your phone bill

either.'' He wished he could talk to her in person. There was so much he wanted to say.

''Take care of yourself,'' she said.

''I will. You too.''

''Okay. And Nick?''

''Yeah?''

''I love you.''

Before he could say anything she hung up.

Nick stared at the phone in his hand. Were his ears working right? She'd just said she loved him. How could she hang up after saying that? He started to dial her number and then thought better of it. She loved him. This was an idea he had to get used to.

Chapter Ten

Nick wandered around in a fog the rest of that day and night as he thought about what Teal had told him. She loved him. Just out of the blue she up and told him that she was in love with him. It was just like her to do something like that. He'd been feeling frustrated and worried about her and then she went and changed all that with three little words. He smiled to himself as he thought about it. One thing he could always say about Teal—she was never boring.

He was still smiling as he went to the hospital the next day. Misty had been with Matt all morning, and it was Nick's turn to give her a break. He knocked on the door before he entered and found his father sitting up in bed. Misty was sitting beside him reading a book out loud.

"There you are," Matt said with relief.

Misty playfully swatted her hand at his arm. "You don't have to sound so happy about my

164

leaving, you know. This is a good book. It won't hurt you to sit and listen to it.''

''Oh, it's not that,'' Matt was quick to explain. ''I've been dying to tell him our news. Since we're all here together now why don't you do the honors.''

Nick tried to act like he didn't know what was coming. ''What news? You look a little bit too excited for it to be bad. Doctors letting you come home soon?'' he guessed.

''We think it's good news, son. Go ahead, Misty.''

A bright pink flush had crept up Misty's cheeks and she looked down in embarrassment. She still wasn't sure of her welcome where Nick was concerned. This could very well set him off again, and she was afraid. ''You tell him, Matt. I think it's your place to do that with your son.''

Matt frowned at her bowed head. She had told him that she and Nick were getting along fine. What was going on that he didn't know about? He hated being in this hospital away from everything. He also hated the way they tried to shield him from everything. It was obvious that Nick had something on his mind. He could tell that just from the silly grin on Nick's face when he'd walked in. He sighed as some of his excitement drained away.

''What gives?'' Nick asked as he focused all of

his attention on his father. He sensed that his father really needed his support now, and he was going to give it to him this time. He'd share in his happiness from here on out. No more running away for him.

Matt smiled at the interested look on Nick's face. "Misty and I are going to have a baby, son."

He looked so contented sitting there as he put his arm around Misty and drew her close. She still wasn't looking at Nick, but the look on his father's face said it all. Nick beamed at him. "Congratulations, dad," he said, feigning surprise. "Another one running around the house will be just what you need."

Misty looked up suspecting that Nick was being sarcastic. She was surprised to see only genuine affection shining in Nick's eyes.

"Misty, I think motherhood already becomes you. There's a glow in your eyes that I don't remember from before. I know you'll make a wonderful mother. Congratulations. I'm happy for you." Nick smiled at her and she couldn't help but smile back.

"Thank you," she answered softly. She was so surprised at his reaction that she couldn't think of anything else to say. She had expected this to be the last straw between the two of them.

Matt cleared his throat, trying to dislodge the

lump of emotion sticking there. "Why don't you go home and get some lunch and rest awhile," he said to Misty. "It's never too soon to start conserving your energy."

Misty laughed and the tension in the room cleared. "I'm pregnant, not sick," she said in exasperation. "I'll be back this evening," she said as she bent to kiss him goodbye.

Nick looked away as his father held her in a loving embrace. When Misty had gone he sat down in her chair next to the bed. "So, I guess you're feeling pretty good, huh?" Nick asked.

"I wish you'd tell those doctors that. They think they have to poke and prod me every time they turn around. There's nothing wrong with me that a little time won't cure."

"I take it that means they're keeping you here for awhile yet."

"They said maybe tomorrow. I guess they're still watching me since that concussion was so bad or something."

"I bet they want to get you rehydrated and strengthened up from that infection you had, too. It won't hurt you to spend another day in bed."

"Everybody's so quick to tell me what won't hurt me," Matt said in disgust.

Nick laughed at his expression. "We're just glad we still have you here with us. It makes us feel better to fuss over you.'' He looked at his father and their eyes met and held.

''It's good to have you home,'' Matt said simply.

Nick grabbed his hand and squeezed it. ''It's good to be home.''

Matt squeezed back and they sat together in shared silence, finally appreciating everything they had together. Matt cleared his throat and wiped his eyes and laughed to clear the emotion that hung in the air. ''So, what brought you in here with that silly look on your face?'' he asked to get them back on even ground.

''What silly look? I just walked in here like normal.''

''You had a lovesick grin on your face. Don't deny it to me—I know what I saw. Where is she and when do I get to meet her?''

Nick looked at him in surprise. He didn't know he'd been that obvious. ''Um . . . well . . . she lives in Colorado. That's where she is. And I don't know exactly when you'll meet her. She can't leave her ranch right now. She has to be there to take care of her herd. They're socked in with a blizzard right now anyway.''

''Rancher, huh?'' he said thoughtfully. ''Is that all you're going to tell me?''

"What do you want to know?" Nick asked in confusion.

"How about her name for starters?" Getting information out of this boy had always been like pulling teeth.

"Oh, yeah. It's Teal. Teal Berringer, and she lives not far from Walden. Her father died this summer, leaving her the ranch, and I've been helping her run it for a few months now."

"What's she look like?"

"She has the most incredible long blond hair," Nick said as he really warmed up to his subject. "And bright green eyes, and she used to teach P.E., so you can imagine that she's built like an athlete. Incredible walk," he added as an afterthought.

Matt could imagine exactly what he was talking about. "You in love with her?"

Nick smiled at him. "Yes," he said in a most definite voice.

Matt looked at him thoughtfully. "She know that?"

"Not exactly," he answered as some of his confidence ebbed away.

"Oh? Why not?"

"We were just kind of . . . well, we sort of were just getting around to that. She had a lot of things to deal with, and—oh, I don't know. I just haven't told her yet.''

Matt nodded his head. ''She in love with you, you think?''

The silly grin was back on his face as he answered. ''Yes, I know she is.''

Matt smiled with him. ''When's the wedding?''

''You're getting ahead of me, dad. There are lots of things to decide before we get around to that.''

''Like what?''

Like what indeed. Nick had to think for a moment. ''Like where we're going to live, and how many children we want to have. That kind of thing.''

''That's easy enough. She's got a ranch that you seem to like. I imagine if she inherited it from her father she isn't going to want to leave. So there you go on that one. Why don't you wait and see how many children you have.''

Nick smiled in amusement. It felt really good to be getting advice from his father. He hadn't realized how much he had missed talking to him like this. Once his mother had died he hadn't really talked to anyone in his family again. ''I remember a time when you wanted me to ranch with you,'' Nick said as he looked down. He still felt like he

needed to be here for his father. He'd wasted too much valuable time as it was.

Matt closed his eyes and leaned back. "You know you always have a place here if you want it," he said softly. "I know you feel guilty for the lost years, and so do I. We really can't go back and do it over again. What we can do is put it behind us, and enjoy the time we have left. I love you, son. I love you enough to let you go. A good woman is too hard to find to just throw her love away. I'd never ask that of you. Why should you ask that of yourself? Airplanes still fly back and forth between here and Colorado don't they?"

An incredible peace stole over Nick as he sat there beside his father. The guilt he'd been holding inside for years finally broke apart and melted away. And with its release he felt whole again. He cleared his throat roughly. "From what I hear, planes still do fly between here and Denver. Thanks, dad."

Matt patted him on the shoulder. "Of course I expect to see you coming off a plane at least twice a year. You've got a little brother or sister that's going to need to know you."

"Bring her to Colorado, dad. We'll teach her to ski."

"Her?" Now that he thought about it, that

sounded nice. ''You know, I'd kind of like to have a daughter myself.''

Nick stood up and hugged his father close. Cars drove by in a hurry outside the hospital and nurses continued to run up and down the halls as they took care of their many duties, but inside Matt's room all was peaceful and quiet. Nick had found his way home.

What a coward she was. She'd told him that she loved him, but she was too afraid to stay on the line and find out what he had to say about it. She half expected him to call her back, but he didn't. She didn't know if that meant he was angry or not. He'd sounded like his old self; maybe that meant he wasn't looking to distance himself from her. Well, she could always hope.

The snow finally stopped, but by the time it left there was a foot and a half of snow on the ground. Teal fought for several hours to put the blade on the front of her pickup. She'd seen her father do it several times, but it was an awkward thing to do by herself. A mechanic she wasn't. She kicked it several times out of frustration until eventually she had it on. She bladed the yard and down the lane to the fence and out to where the hay was stacked. It was kind of fun once she got the hang of it.

Now that she was doing these things for herself, she looked back on her fear and uncertainty as a different lifetime. She'd been so afraid that she couldn't do it without Joe. What a laugh. The ranch had never looked this good when he was taking care of it. She knew that her newfound self-confidence came from Nick. He had taught her many things about ranching, but the thing she'd drawn from him the most was self-confidence. He believed in her, making it possible for her to believe in herself. She knew her father would like the way things were going. It made her feel good to think of him watching her. The thing she missed the most was telling him all about what she was doing.

The only thing she felt like she'd left undone was Joe Andrews. His case still hadn't come up, and she wished she could put it behind her. She hadn't seen hide nor hair of him, making it easy for her to forget about him most of the time. She felt like she needed to put everything in order, kind of like spring cleaning, getting rid of all the old trash and things that weren't necessary to keep anymore. She didn't really care anymore what happened to him; she just wanted to put it behind her and close the door on that part of her life.

Millie thought that Teal needed to call Nick again and find out what was going on. She'd been astounded when Teal had told her that she'd hung up after telling him of her love. Teal just shrugged it off. Telling him over the phone probably hadn't been a good idea in the first place. It was too impersonal. Besides that there was the cost of the long distance call hanging over their heads, and they never felt like they had time to say what they really wanted to anyway.

She'd gotten it off her chest and that was all that mattered for now. She was at peace with her decision. She'd put the ball in Nick's court, and now all she had to do was wait and see what he did with it.

She didn't begin to worry until a whole week had passed without a word from him. What was going on? she wondered. She wondered if the woman she had talked to on the telephone had anything to do with it. She came up with all sorts of weird ideas to explain her away, but still had no real clue what she was doing there. Maybe hanging up hadn't been the right thing to do after all.

Chapter Eleven

Two weeks later, the strain was beginning to take its toll on Teal. Dark circles were ringing her eyes, evidence of many sleepless nights. Her clothes were beginning to hang on her as she lost pound after pound. Food didn't sound in the least bit appetizing. She made it a point not to be in the house most of the day, avoiding Millie and all of her efforts to coax her into eating something. She found plenty of things to occupy her time outdoors. It warmed up a little bit after the storm, and she saddled up a horse and rode around to check the cattle and make sure they were all healthy.

She was riding along the fence checking for weak spots when she noticed a pickup driving down to the barn. She put her left hand above her eyes to shield the glare of the sun, but it was too far away to tell who it was. She expected to see it driving away again when whoever it was found she wasn't around. After awhile she forgot about

175

it as she lost herself in the rhythm of her horse and the creak of her saddle. It was so peaceful and quiet up here that she couldn't imagine living anywhere else ever again.

The mountains looked majestic with snow covering every inch of the craggy peaks. Sagebrush and willows were the only thing within miles that were brave enough to poke their heads above the blanket of white. Her horse was crunching along as his hooves broke through the hardened snow and touched the ground. He had to pick his feet up high to move along, and the going was slow. Teal didn't mind as she enjoyed this winter wonderland for all it was worth. It was the only thing that could take her mind off Nick. The all-consuming force of nature was the only thing powerful enough to wrench her out of her self-absorption.

She was working her way back towards the barn when a weird noise made her rein in her horse. A steady crunching and swishing noise was coming from up ahead, but there were too many willows in the way to see what was making it. She remembered that she had seen several of the cattle over this way on her way out, and she moved forward again at ease.

She moved up to higher ground with the fence-line and stopped in astonishment. Her horse whinnied and Nick turned toward the sound. He immediately kicked his horse into a gallop and was in front of her in seconds. Teal just stared at him with her mouth hanging open.

"Good thing it's wintertime," he said.

Teal just looked at him stupidly. She couldn't believe he was real. She blinked and rubbed her eyes, but he was still there. "Why?" she asked in confusion.

"The flies and mosquitoes would be building nests in your mouth otherwise."

It took her a second to understand what he meant. Once it hit her she quickly closed her mouth. Nick smiled at her, but all she could do was stare.

"Don't I even get a hello?" he asked. He was suddenly glad that she had told him that she loved him. Otherwise he would be feeling more than a little out of his depth with her just sitting and staring at him. She didn't even look glad to see him.

"I'm sorry," she apologized. "I guess I don't understand. What are you doing here?"

Nick relaxed back in his saddle. Obviously this was going to take a little more than he had expected. "My father is recovering nicely. He's been home for over a week, and they don't really need me hanging around anymore. He's so happy with his wife and the thought of their new baby that he's going to recover a lot faster than the doctors thought he would. I figured my employer would be wanting me back to do some work by now.''

''Wife? Baby?'' What was he talking about?

Nick burst out laughing at her expression. ''All right—I know I owe you an explanation. I left home five years ago because my father remarried. I didn't like Misty one bit, and her being a year younger than me didn't help either. I couldn't believe that my father would do that to my mother.'' He sighed thinking about it. ''Well, after listening to you and watching you handle your father's death, I learned a few things. I had always thought that it was Misty I didn't like and that my father was betraying my mother's memory, but I was wrong. It wasn't Misty. Any woman would have gotten the same reaction. I just didn't handle my mother's death very well, and I took it out on my father. He got tired of me baiting Misty one day and we had a huge argument. I couldn't believe that he was defending her to me, and I left. If it weren't for you, I might never have gone back. Anyway, to make a long story short, my father and I worked things out, and I even get along with Misty now. She's grown up a lot. They're so in love with one another that I can't believe that I didn't see it five years ago. In fact, they're having a baby. I told my father to bring my little sister out here and we'd teach her to ski.''

''That must have been the woman that answered the phone that day,'' Teal murmured to herself.

Nick nodded and waited for her to say something else.

''I thought you were going to stay out there. Now that you and your father are getting along, you probably want to work with your family.''

''I have to be honest, I entertained the idea for awhile. My father made me realize that no amount of guilt was going to change anything. I don't need to stay there to make up for the years apart. We're a family again, and that's all that matters.''

Teal was almost afraid to ask what had brought him back here. She'd told him that she loved him, but she had never once heard him say the same thing. He'd talked about having a relationship, but what did that mean to a man like Nick?

Nick dismounted from his horse and looked up at Teal. ''Come down from there.'' He held up his arms and waited for her. She swung her leg over and landed directly in front of him. He placed both of his hands on her horse, effectively trapping her within his arms. ''How does that partnership idea grab you?''

His voice had dropped into a sensual tone that rippled through her in waves. She shivered and closed her eyes, swaying against him. He steadied her by locking his fingers in her hair as he waited for her answer. She opened her eyes and was stunned by the feeling emanating from his expressive brown eyes. "Are we talking about business?" she managed to ask in a raspy whisper.

"You know we're not."

She looked up at him and waited. She'd told him that she loved him—now it was his turn. Her love was shining out of her eyes and it was all she could do keep from kissing him, but still she waited.

As Nick held her gaze he sensed that she wasn't going to answer him. He hadn't seen her for so long that he was content for a moment just to stand and drink in the sight of her. Her eyes were shining with emotion and her cheeks were bright red from the brisk afternoon air; he lightly ran his finger underneath one of her eyes as he noticed the dark tinge for the first time. Her cheeks were thinner, almost gaunt, and as she trembled underneath his touch he realized how much she had been suffering. Everything inside him melted at the realization of how much she loved him. He smiled tenderly. "I think you were right about that mountain magic after all."

"What makes you say that?" she whispered in a voice shaky with emotion.

"I got away from the mountains only to realize that I had to come back."

"For the ranch?"

"For you."

Teal closed her eyes as she swayed toward him again.

"I love you," he whispered just before he claimed her lips in a passionate kiss.

She opened like a flower underneath him and wildly threw her arms around his neck, clinging to him fervently. He held her tightly to him for some time before he was willing to let her go. She smiled up at him breathlessly realizing that all of her dreams had come true. "How does a fifty/fifty partnership sound to you?" she asked.

"Are you talking about business?"

"I'm talking about life."

He startled her as he dropped down to one knee and removed a box from his jacket. He removed the golden engagement band from the box and held it on the end of his finger. Grasping her left hand lightly, he looked up at her expectantly. "Will you marry me?"

Her cheeks were wet with tears but she didn't even notice as she replied, "I promise to love you for the rest of my life, Nick Marcus. Yes, I'll marry you."

He slid the ring onto her finger before standing

up to embrace her again. As he held her against his chest and she listened to the steady beating of his heart, she realized that she had found her own magic in these mountains—a magic she had never before dreamed possible.